A

GW01086736

In-Laws, Outlaws, and Other People (That Should Be Shot)

by Steve Franco

A SAMUEL FRENCH ACTING EDITION

SMELL THE CHEESE

SAMUEL FRENCH
FOUNDED 1830

SAMUELFRENCH.COM

ISBN 978-0-87440-894-2   Printed in U.S.A.   #B2268

MUSIC USE NOTE

Licensees are solely responsible for obtaining formal written permission from copyright owners to use copyrighted music in the performance of this play and are strongly cautioned to do so. If no such permission is obtained by the licensee, then the licensee must use only original music that the licensee owns and controls. Licensees are solely responsible and liable for all music clearances and shall indemnify the copyright owners of the play and their licensing agent, Samuel French, Inc., against any costs, expenses, losses and liabilities arising from the use of music by licensees.

IMPORTANT BILLING AND CREDIT
REQUIREMENTS

All producers of *IN-LAWS, OUTLAWS, AND OTHER PEOPLE (THAT SHOULD BE SHOT) must* give credit to the Author of the Play in all programs distributed in connection with performances of the Play, and in all instances in which the title of the Play appears for the purposes of advertising, publicizing or otherwise exploiting the Play and/or a production. The name of the Author *must* appear on a separate line on which no other name appears, immediately following the title and *must* appear in size of type not less than fifty percent of the size of the title type.

IN-LAWS, OUTLAWS, AND OTHER PEOPLE (THAT SHOULD BE SHOT)
had its World Premiere on November 20, 2010 in Salem, Virginia at
Theatre Glenvar High. The performance was directed by Steve Franco.
The cast was as follows:

DAD . . . . Cory Mitchell

BETH . . . . .Ann Marie Noell

MRS. DRAPER . . . . Katie Holland

BUNNY . . . . .Haley Morrison

BUD . . . . Wes Murphy

TRACY . . . . .Susan Clark

AUNT ROSE . . . . Callie Thompson

UNCLE LEO . . . . .Will Dunkenberger

TONY . . . . Alex Kelly

VINNY . . . . .Troy Fryling

PAUL . . . . .Chris Bell

EMILY . . . . Megan Grisso

MRS. WAKOWSKI . . . . .Elizabeth Sherer

CHRISTMAS CAROLERS . . . . Abby Garland, Marina Hafey,
Julia Holland, Rachel Johnson

JANET . . . . Kayla Ellis

OFFICER HENLEY . . . . .Bryce Mallette

CHARACTERS

DAD
BETH
MRS. DRAPER
BUNNY
BUD
TRACY
AUNT ROSE
UNCLE LEO
TONY
VINNY
PAUL
EMILY
MRS. WAKOWSKI
CHRISTMAS CAROLERS
JANET
OFFICER HENLEY

SETTING

A modest, Upper Middle Class home in the Fiske Terrace area of Brooklyn, New York

TIME

ACT I: 6pm on Christmas Eve, it is snowing heavily
ACT II: Later that evening

AUTHOR'S NOTES

It would be easy to play these roles as caricatures, rather than characters – resist this temptation. The fun in this show comes from how real each of these personality types are to people that we each may know. If you have any questions, please feel free to contact Mr. Franco via publications@samuelfrench.com.

For my wife Ann, whose laughter lights up a room

ACT ONE

Scene One: The Preparations

(As the scene opens we see a split box set with a living room on the stage right side and a dining room on the stage left side. The living room is neither overly formal, nor overly casual, but is a mixture of the two. It has a bay window in the far down right position and an entrance door somewhat farther upper right. The upstage central wall has a doorway that leads to a hallway and a bathroom. The upstage central wall is also divided by a portion of flat that comes down perpendicular to the front of stage – but only about four feet [so as to give the audience the impression of two separate rooms]. That small flat has a door that separates the living room from the dining room. The dining room side of the set is a formal room with a large table and eight matching chairs. It is beautifully decorated in a classic style. The stage left wall has one door near the center that leads to the kitchen.)

(It is 6:00 pm on Christmas Eve and **DAD** *is scurrying around trying to get everything set for the family dinner.* **BETH** *is down the hall in her room. Snow is seen falling outside the bay window.)*

DAD. Beth, hurry up honey, I need you to come in here and help me.

BETH. Dad, I am trying to fix my hair!

DAD. Your hair can wait – hurry up.

BETH. *(irritated)* What!?

DAD. Your mother called – she wants you to check on the ham.

BETH. Whataya mean, "check on the ham"?

DAD. I don't know, sweetheart – I guess check to see if it's done.

BETH. Who am I, Martha Stewart? I don't know anything about ham. I don't eat meat.

DAD. Since when?

BETH. Aaaaaah, I swear! You never listen to a word that I say. I told you months ago that I was becoming a vegetarian.

DAD. Stop swearing – and could you go back to your roots and maybe pretend you're checking on *last year's* ham?

BETH. DAD, I DON'T KNOW A THING ABOUT THE READINESS OF HAM!!!

DAD. Fine. We'll just give the whole family salmonella as a Christmas present.

BETH. Can I choose which ones to poison?!

DAD. Beth, don't start.

BETH. I'm just speaking the truth. Don't pretend that there aren't certain family members that you'd just love to smother in their sleep.

DAD. *(sarcastically)* It's easy to see that you're filled with the peace, love, and joy of the Christmas spirit.

BETH. *Christmas*, I love. But when our relatives come, there's no peace and thus: no joy!

DAD. There are folks that would kill to be in a family like ours.

BETH. And others who want to *kill* a family like ours.

DAD. Just what is it about our family that you don't like?

BETH. It'd be faster to tell you what I *do* like.

(Dad's cell phone rings and he pauses to answer.)

DAD. *(to* **BETH***)* Go get the ham and sit it on the dining room table – and don't forget to put down a trivet. *(to his wife)* Hello…Hi. Sweetheart…no, not yet…

yes…Well, we're working on it. Mmm-hmm. She says she doesn't know…Okay. *(to* **BETH***)* Get out the meat thermometer.

BETH. The what?

DAD. The MEAT THER-MOM-E-TER.

BETH. I'm not an immigrant – I speak English. I just don't know what a *(mocking him)* MEAT THER-MOM-E-TER is!

DAD. *(into phone)* Hang on sweetheart – I need to get the thermometer. Here, talk to your mom.

(He hands her the phone and goes into the kitchen and we hear him digging through the drawers. He re-enters and grabs the phone.)

(to his wife) Where is it?…Well, why in the world do you keep it there?

(to **BETH***)* Go in the kitchen, open the cabinet and get the Crisco off the second shelf – the thermometer is in the Crisco can.

BETH. Why's it in there?

DAD. Because your mom is neurotic – just go.

*(***BETH*** *exits, less than enthused.)*

Yes honey, we will…no…yes, I did…sweetheart, the ham may be overcooking as we speak…Great… All right, I love you too. Have a safe flight – we'll say prayers for you. Okay, bye.

*(***BETH*** *enters carrying the thermometer.)*

BETH. Here.

DAD. *(writing info down on a tablet)* Just jab it in the ham and give me a reading.

BETH. Eeeeeew, I am not "jabbing it in" – that's disgusting.

DAD. What's disgusting about it?!

BETH. Because I told you – I HATE MEAT!

DAD. You've always eaten meat. Since when is meat suddenly so horrid that you can't stick a thermometer in it and tell me the temperature?

BETH. Since I decided meat is *murder.*

DAD. "Meat is murder"...You've been talking with that Wakowski boy again haven't you?!

BETH. What do you have against Paul Wakowski?

DAD. He's a fruit loop for starters. The kid has blue hair.

BETH. So does Aunt Rose, but you let me talk to her.

DAD. You know what I'm talking about – now back to the ham. How is meat "murder"?

BETH. They had to kill that pig to get the ham. I can't eat anything that was living.

DAD. You eat corn – it was living. You eat salad – all that lettuce was once living. What's it matter?

BETH. That's different.

DAD. How?

BETH. Vegetables don't have eyes that look up at you all sad when you're about to kill them.

DAD. Potatoes have eyes.

BETH. Very funny. Vegetables don't cry out in pain when you hurt them.

DAD. Oh, I see. It's about the screaming...what if the pig was mute? Would it be okay to kill it then?

BETH. You are such a jerk!

DAD. *(laughing)* Oh, you bark-eaters are such fun to mess with! Here, hand me the thermometer.

(He pushes it into the ham and then begins to imitate a pig speaking.)

"Ahhhhh – that hurts! Help me Bethy Won Kenobi, you're my only hope!"

BETH. *(unenthused)* I hate you some days.

DAD. *(still laughing)* Oh, lighten up – it's Christmas Eve. *(looks down at thermometer)* What's it say?

BETH. Can't you read it, Mr. Wise Guy?

DAD. No, I left my glasses upstairs – what's it say?

BETH. It's still moving up – kind of slow – but it's moving. What's it supposed to say?

DAD. For pork, at least a hundred and seventy degrees.

BETH. How in the world do you know this stuff?

DAD. Well, you know…you pick up a few things in life, you live a little, and you learn a little and –

BETH. Mom told you, didn't she?

DAD. Yeah, pretty much.

BETH. Shoot, it's past one seventy! I guess that means it's done and we won't poison the carnivores. *(snaps her fingers)* Better luck next year…

DAD. Great! Put it back in the oven on warm and then help me with the rugs.

BETH. What are we doing with the rugs?

DAD. We need to move the ones in front of the doors?

BETH. Why?

DAD. So that your Aunt Rose doesn't trip when she goes from room to room.

BETH. Aunt Rose? Aw, Dad – why didn't you tell me *she* was coming?!

DAD. Because I knew that would be your reaction.

BETH. She never stops talking. Ever.

DAD. She's sweet and we are blessed to have her.

BETH. She should have a job on talk radio – she could make a fortune.

DAD. Well, I will admit that sometimes she does tend to get a little…wordy.

BETH. Calling her a little wordy is like calling *War and Peace* "a little long".

DAD. Sweetheart, we'll get through it fine. Just let her talk, and ask you a few questions, pinch your cheeks a couple of times, and before you know it – everyone will be on their way. Then you can sit down and enjoy a great big tofu burger with some gently plucked tomatoes that have no voice and –

(She picks up a cloth napkin and sticks it is his mouth. He laughs as he removes the napkin.)

BETH. Who else did you invite to this thing?

DAD. "This *thing?*" Sweetheart, its Christmas Eve dinner –

BETH. Don't try to distract me by changing the subject – who'd you invite?

DAD. ...Uncle Bud and Aunt Bunny.

BETH. Aw, Dad – why????

DAD. Beth, they are family –

BETH. Who in the world names their children "Bud" and "Bunny?!"

DAD. They're nick-names, sweetheart.

BETH. They're both in their forties – couldn't they start using their real names?!?

DAD. Not likely.

BETH. Why?!

DAD. Well, his parents named him Rudolf.

BETH. *(laughs sarcastically)* That's great–I hope he brings Donner and Blitzen! No wonder he goes by Bud.

DAD. It gets better.

BETH. Okay, I have to know – what's Aunt Bunny's real name?

DAD. *(trying to keep a straight face)* Hortense.

BETH. "Hortense?!" ...Okay, maybe "Bunny" isn't so bad.

DAD. So is that why you don't want them here – because they have bad names?

BETH. No...it's just that he's a redneck. She's a space invader.

DAD. What makes him a redneck?

BETH. You know, he wears cammo and he hunts animals.

DAD. What's wrong with hunting?

BETH. Nothing, if you're Davy Crockett. *He's* from New Jersey! New Jersey's not supposed to have rednecks.

DAD. I'll let you in on something: *everywhere* has rednecks – New Jersey, more so than some other places.

BETH. I just hope he doesn't show up with a plate full o' something he just killed. I can't eat anything that he shot.

DAD. Oh, I wouldn't worry about that. If Bud shows up with a dish – I'm sure it will be something that he ran over on the way here. *(laughs as she cringes)*

BETH. That is disgusting.

DAD. Just what exactly is a "space invader?"

BETH. One of those people that stands way too close to you when they're talking. She does it all the time. The smell of her cheap perfume could melt cheese.

DAD. I suppose this would be a bad time to mention that your cousin Tracy is coming.

BETH. "Terrific Tracy?" Why are they bringing her – didn't she escape the asylum?

DAD. Maybe it was just a three day pass.

(They both chuckle.)

Either way, she'll still be here. Now, could you please go and put the ham back in the oven?

BETH. Why don't I move the rugs – you move the meat?

DAD. Suit yourself.

(He crosses into the dining room, picks up the ham and exits into the kitchen. **BETH** *begins rolling up the small rug in front of the door when the doorbell rings. Before she can stand up to answer, the door opens and* **MRS. DRAPER** *enters nearly stepping on* **BETH***)*

BETH. Whoa!

MRS. DRAPER. Well, heavens-to-Betsy, Beth – what are you doing down there?

BETH. The better question is: what are *you* doing *in here?!*

MRS. DRAPER. I came over to borrow a cup of sugar.

BETH. You couldn't wait for me to answer the bell?

MRS. DRAPER. The last time I rang the bell, I waited and waited, and it was forever before anyone answered the door. I didn't want to freeze to death in the snow.

BETH. Mom probably saw it was you and was pretending she wasn't home.

MRS. DRAPER. *(misses the insult)* Oh my, aren't you the funny one.

BETH. That's what they tell me.

(**DAD** *enters from the kitchen, through the dining room, and into the living room.*)

DAD. Beth, who was at the – Oh, hello Mrs. Draper. How are you this evening?

MRS. DRAPER. I am wonderful, just wonderful, but I am in need of a little sugar. Do you think that you could spare a cup? I've no interest in driving in this mess.

DAD. Of course. Beth, go and get Mrs. Draper two cups of sugar.

BETH. She only asked for one.

DAD. She may need a little extra and we wouldn't want her to have to come back…

(*He waves her off. She rolls her eyes and exits.*)

Are you all ready for Christmas?

MRS. DRAPER. Other than this last batch of cookies – yes. But apparently you aren't.

DAD. What do you mean?

MRS. DRAPER. Well, I don't want to sound like a busybody, but…well, Thomas…*someone* hasn't turned on their lights yet and it's been dark for well over thirty minutes.

DAD. What?

MRS. DRAPER. Your Christmas lights aren't on and it's already dark…You know how the neighborhood coalition feels about uniformity. Someone isn't conforming…

(**BETH** *enters with the sugar.*)

DAD. We've had a busy day – Janet is in Vermont on business and we have relatives coming over for dinner and –

MRS. DRAPER. (*condescending*) We're all busy Thomas – it's Christmas Eve.

BETH. Here you go – sweets for the…for you.

MRS. DRAPER. Well, I suppose I'd better get over there and finish those cookies while you tend to those lights. Merry Christmas Eve!

(She exits in a hurry.)

DAD. *(as she's exiting)* Merry Christmas Eve…*(under his breath, still smiling)* I hope you slip on the walk and fracture something.

BETH. Now who's Ebenezer?

DAD. *(smiling)* Bah humbug!

(Lights fade to blue. End of scene.)

Scene Two: Relatively Speaking

(As the lights come up onstage, we see the Christmas tree lit and **DAD** *crossing to the door. He welcomes in* **BUNNY, BUD,** *and* **TRACY. BETH** *is seated in a chair, texting.)*

DAD. Hello! Come on in.

BUNNY. Have you ever seen such a snow in your life? And on Christmas Eve. Isn't it beautiful?!

BUD. It's a road hazard, that's all it is.

BUNNY. Oh, stop your bellyachin', you ole Grinch.

DAD. *(helps* **BUNNY** *with her coat)* Here let me take that.

BUD. It's slick as a whale turd out there.

BETH. …that paints a lovely mental picture…

DAD. *(shoots her an irritated look)* Glad you made it safe, Bud.

BUD. Just barely – people drive like idiots in this stuff.

BUNNY. You think people drive like idiots when it's *not* snowing.

BUD. That's because they do. They just drive like bigger ones when it is.

BUNNY. Bud Nester if you don't stop complaining – Santa's going to leave you a sack of coal for Christmas.

BUD. Good, I can use it to warm up my feet.

DAD. Well settle in and get warm. Hello Tracy, it's great to see you! Beth, why don't you and Tracy go into the kitchen and get everyone something to drink.

(As **BUD** *begins to speak, we see* **BETH** *and* **TRACY** *roll their eyes and then mouth out every word that* **BUD** *says in such a way that we get the feeling they've heard this old joke many times before.)*

BUD. Make mine a scotch and soda – hold the soda.

(He laughs at himself as if it's the first time he's ever said it.)

BUNNY. Never mind your uncle, sweetheart – he doesn't even drink alcohol. He just thinks that line is hysterical.

BETH & TRACY. *(together, quietly)* He's the only one…

DAD. *(clears his throat intentionally)* Go.

(They exit.)

BUNNY. Okay Tom, why's my baby sister not here to greet me?!

DAD. She's been in Vermont on business and had a late flight out. She called a while ago and said that her flight was delayed while they cleared the runways and de-iced the plane. But she should be here soon.

BUNNY. Vermont? On Christmas Eve?! What's so important in Vermont?

BUD. Nothing's important in Vermont! Inns and maple syrup – it's all they got.

DAD. And covered bridges.

BUD. Who cares about covered bridges? That's just one more thing you gotta keep up with.

BUNNY. Why's she there?

DAD. Her firm was hired to oversee the renovation and repair of five different bridges across the state.

BUD. What's I say? – just more to keep up with! A fella'd hafta have a screw loose to wanna live in Vermont.

BUNNY. Vermont is a beautiful state –

BUD. No it's not – it's a rat hole! They only have two seasons in Vermont: Winter and late winter.

BUNNY. Whata you know about it?

BUD. Plenty, you have the same two seasons!

BUNNY. If you ever want "spring thaw" – you better start behaving!

(BETH and TRACY enter from kitchen carrying glasses for everyone. BETH crosses to BUD and BUNNY and hands them their drinks.)

BETH. Here you go.

BUNNY. Thank you dear. *(sips)* Mmmmm, that's good – what is it?

BETH. Christmas punch.

BUD. *(looks down into his cup, suspect)* What's in it?

BETH. The usual: sprite and juice and stuff.

BUD. So this punch is made with stuff that didn' have *any* *punch*?! *(He chuckles to himself.)*

BETH. *(snidely)* Yes. It's also made with pineapple juice – which has neither pine nor apple in it. So I'd say it's a fraud beverage all the way around.

DAD. *(can't resist)* Beth...

BETH. What?

DAD. Hold the punch lines.

*(**DAD**, **BUD** and **BUNNY** laugh at his pun.)*

BUNNY. So how's our little Bethy doing?

BETH. I'm fine.

BUNNY. How's school – are you making good grades?

BETH. Yes – good enough, I guess.

DAD. She's being modest. Beth has a 4.0 – despite the fact that she doesn't know what a meat thermometer is.

BETH: Yes, but I do know *not* to end a sentence in a preposition.

BUNNY. That's just wonderful, Beth. Tracy has a 4.15 – *(to **DAD**)* she takes weighted classes you know. When you two were little, I just knew you were both going to grow up to be brilliant.

BUD. *(burps loudly)* Yep, apple don't fall far from the tree, huh?!

TRACY. *(to **BETH**)* Praise God it falls.

BUNNY. Tracy, tell Uncle Thomas your big honor.

TRACY. Mom, please.

BUNNY. Go on – tell him!

TRACY. *(embarrassed)* I got the lead in the winter musical.

DAD. That's great, Tracy –

BUNNY. Go on – tell him what show it is!!

TRACY. Mom, would you please stop – no one cares.

DAD. That's not true – I care. What show is it?

TRACY. *Annie Get Your Gun.*

DAD. Really?!? My senior year, I was "Frank" in our production of *Annie Get Your Gun.*

TRACY. You were a Thespian?

DAD. Oh yes, I've always liked girls.

BETH. *(rolls her eyes in disgust)* Ha, ha.

TRACY. I had no idea you acted.

BETH. He acts up – it's embarrassing.

BUD. Haven't you two figured that out yet? Embarrassing you's part of the plan – it's pay back for all the times you embarrassed us when you were little.

TRACY. Mission accomplished.

BUNNY. Oh my goodness, I remember this one time at Bible school when you took your dress and –

TRACY. MOM!!! Don't even go there.

(The doorbell rings.)

DAD. Must be Rose and Leo.

(He crosses to the door. As he opens it, we see **MRS. DRAPER** *standing there with a sour look on her face.)*

MRS. DRAPER. I suppose the feelings of your neighbors aren't really that important on Christmas Eve now are they?

DAD. The lights!! Oh crud, I am so sorry – I got sidetracked and they completely slipped my mind.

MRS. DRAPER. That's pretty apparent.

DAD. I'll cut them on right now – my Christmas present to you.

MRS. DRAPER. *(to* **BUNNY***)* Excuse Thomas' rudeness – you are...?

BUNNY. Bunny.

MRS. DRAPER. "Bunny"?

BUNNY. It's an old nickname.

MRS. DRAPER. One could only hope. *(smiles arrogantly)*

BUNNY. I'm his sister-in-law. And you...?

MRS. DRAPER. I'm their next-door neighbor – Sue Draper.

DAD. *(crosses back to center, smiling)* Lights are on and reflecting in the snow. Isn't it beautiful?!

MRS. DRAPER. It's a road hazard – that's what it is.

BUD. What'd I say?!

MRS. DRAPER. I've always thought that a man'd have to be an idiot to get out in a mess like this... *(She looks down her nose at* **BUD** *and* **BUNNY.***)* and I can see my theory is accurate. Well Thomas, thank you for finally fulfilling your neighborly duties – even if it was under duress. I'd better hurry home – Theodore'll think I got lost. *(crosses to door)*

BETH. *(quietly to* **TRACY***)* He's not that lucky.

DAD. Thank you for looking out for us Mrs. Draper – we don't know what we'd do without you. *(opens door)*

BETH. Live in *peace.*

MRS. DRAPER. All sheep need a shepherd.

(She exits.)

BETH. *(loudly)* Baaaaaaaaaaaaaaah.

DAD. Goodnight. *(closes door)* Beth, that was rude!

BETH. She's rude! *(imitating* **MRS. DRAPER***)* "One can oooonly hooope."

DAD. "Do unto others" – even when they're rude to you.

TRACY. Having her as a neighbor must be a real test.

BETH. Everyone has their cross to bear.

DAD. She's not that bad.

BETH. She's not that *good* either.

DAD: She's just a concerned neighbor.

BETH. She's just a nosy neighbor. Big difference.

BUNNY. Well, let's not let a little rudeness get in the way of our celebration. What can we help you with?

DAD. I think we have everything set. We just need Aunt Rose and Uncle Leo and Janet, and all the family will be here.

BUNNY. I completely forgot the gifts. Bud, go to the van and get 'em.

BUD. It's snowing like crazy out there!

BUNNY. Good, then you can follow your tracks back to the door and we won't have to worry about you getting lost.

(**BUD** *grumbles, gets his coat and starts to exit.*)

DAD. Hang on Bud, I'll help you.

(*He gets his coat and exits as well.*)

BUNNY. Something certainly does smell good back there. What is it?

BETH. *(with disdain)* Ham.

BUNNY. Oh, I looooove ham. The smell of it takes me back to when I was a little girl. My Pawpaw'd go out and butcher a hog fresh for us every time we'd visit. Sometimes he'd even let me chop off the feet.

(**BETH** *looks mortified.*)

I'd take 'em and chase your mother around with 'em.

(**BETH** *is horrified and is cringing at the thought.*)

Then my Granny Lester'd skin him – while Pawpaw pulled out the guts. Sheeew-wee it smelled – worse than a sewer.

(**BETH** *looks like she might throw up.*)

Then they'd take this great, big, skewer and jab it right through him!! Then they'd –

BETH. *(jumps up and runs for the bathroom)* I think I'm gonna be sick.

BUNNY. *(to **TRACY**)* Did I say something wrong.

TRACY. Wouldn't be the first time...I'll go check on her.

(*Exits through upstage center doorway. The stage right door opens and we see **BUD** and **DAD** carrying gifts. They are covered in snow.*)

BUNNY. Careful Bud, you're tracking snow all over the place!

BUD. That's what happens when you send someone out in the snow – they track it back in!

DAD. Don't worry about that; let's just get these gifts under the tree.

BUNNY. I sure hope this stuff lets up like the weather man said. I don't want Janet to miss Christmas Eve dinner.

DAD. I know what you mean. They weren't calling for more than an inch or two, but there's at least 6 inches out there already.

(The doorbell rings.)

BUNNY. I'll get it.

(She crosses to door and opens it revealing **AUNT ROSE** *and* **UNCLE LEO.***)*

AUNT ROSE. Anybody home?!

BUNNY. Leo, Rose, it's great to see you – come on in!

UNCLE LEO. Merry Christmas!

BUNNY. Now Leo, you know you're supposed to say "Happy Holidays."

UNCLE LEO. *(curmudgeon)* I'm not celebrating "holi-*days*" – I'm celebrating Christmas – singular. So I'm gonna say "Merry Christmas" – I don't care if it's correct or not.

AUNT ROSE. Leo's always had a problem with authority.

UNCLE LEO. I do not have a problem with authority – I have a problem with being told what I'm allowed to do.

*(***BETH*** and ***TRACY*** enter.)*

BUD. Can't blame you there, Leo.

TRACY. Hi, Uncle Leo! *(rushes across room to hug him)*

UNCLE LEO: How's my Tracy?!

AUNT ROSE. Come here and gimme a hug!

UNCLE LEO. *(to* **BETH***)* Come over here and let me get a look at you.

*(***BETH*** crosses and turns sideways as ***UNCLE LEO*** gives her a hug.)*

AUNT ROSE. *(reaches over and pinches both girls' cheeks)* You two are getting' ta be such big ladies – aren't they, Leo?

UNCLE LEO. You're certainly growing up, but I learned a long time ago that it's not wise to tell a gal she's "getting big."

TRACY. You're a smart man, Uncle Leo.

BETH. We could use some of that around here.

BUD. *(with his hat sideways, to* **DAD***)* What's she talkin' about?

AUNT ROSE. This reminds me of the Christmases we used to have when I was a little girl –

BETH. *(to* **TRACY***)* Here we go…

AUNT ROSE. It used to snow every year – just like clockwork.

TRACY. You always had a white Christmas?

UNCLE LEO. Beige actually.

TRACY. You had beige snow?

UNCLE LEO. Of course – it was New York. We haven't had white snow here in the last hundred years.

BETH. Wasn't Irving Berlin from New York?

UNCLE LEO. Oh no, Irving was from Belarus – but later he moved to New York.

BETH. So then why'd he write "White Christmas?"

UNCLE LEO. Because the man could smell a "hit." Do you think he'd have reached number one with "I'm dreaming of a *Beige* Christmas?"

BETH. No, I guess not.

UNCLE LEO. He had a nose for business. Irving could smell two things faster than anybody I ever met: he could smell a pastrami sandwich and he could smell a hit. And he rarely passed on either one.

TRACY. You knew Irving Berlin?!

UNCLE LEO. Of course I did. We used to have lunch everyday at Schnellendahl's Delicatessen on forty-second street.

AUNT ROSE. Oh Leo, stop stretching the story – you only ate there twice a week and Schnellendahl's was on forty-fourth street right next to Heppner's.

UNCLE LEO. Stretchin' – who's stretchin? I'm telling the God's honest truth. And Schnellendahl's didn't move to forty-fourth street until 1946 – after the war. Irving wrote "White Christmas" in 1940.

AUNT ROSE. Are you sure?

UNCLE LEO. Of course I'm sure. And you know where he wrote it?

EVERYONE. Where?!

UNCLE LEO. He wrote it beside his swimming pool.

DAD. Are you serious?

UNCLE LEO. Serious as a heart attack. The man was golden I'm tellin' yas. He wrote the greatest selling Christmas song of all time, sitting beside his *pool* on a ninety five degree summer day.

BETH. No way.

UNCLE LEO. God's honest truth – the man was a genius, I'm tellin' yas. A genius!

BUNNY. Wow – I never knew that you guys knew Irving Berlin. Tell us more…

UNCLE LEO. Well one time, me and Irving…

(Lights fade to black as the scene ends.)

Scene Three: A Knock at the Door

(As the family mills around waiting to take their seats,
DAD *hangs up the phone and speaks to everyone.)*

DAD. Okay everybody, Janet's flight is taking off in just a few minutes. She's obviously not going to make it for dinner, but with any luck – she'll be here in time to exchange presents. She wanted me to tell you she's sorry she's missing dinner.

BETH. Who in the world is knocking on the door on Christmas Eve?

DAD. I'll get it Ebenezer. *(crosses to door)*

BETH. Why didn't they ring the bell?

DAD. Maybe they didn't see the button. *(looks out peep hole)*

BETH. Who is it?

DAD. It's two guys...but I don't recognize them.

BETH. Well don't open the door – they could be robbers!

DAD. Robbers don't generally knock before they enter.

(He opens the door and we see two men standing almost inside the doorway. They are covered in snow and somewhat shifty. When they speak, there is no doubt that they are from the Bronx.)

DAD. Good evening, can I help you?

TONY. Yeah, uh...we was drivin down the street here and slid and smashed right into your fountain.

DAD. We don't have a fountain.

*(**TONY** points a gun at **DAD**'s chest.)*

TONY. What a coincidence – we don't got a car.

(He pushes his way into the living room and immediately takes control, his partner in crime following close behind.)

Okay everybody shut it and listen up. We're sorry to be bustin' in on ya's like this, bein' its Christmas Eve and all, but me an' Vinny ain't real interested in goin' to jail.

AUNT ROSE. *(loudly)* Oh my goodness, he's got a gun!

UNCLE LEO. We can see that, Rose.

AUNT ROSE. And the other one's got a bag!

UNCLE LEO. We can see that too, Rose.

AUNT ROSE. –And we don't even know them!

UNCLE LEO. You have an amazing grasp for the obvious.

AUNT ROSE. Oh my word, we're being taken hostage!!!

TONY. Lady – shut it!!

DAD. Calm down, sir –

TONY. *(counters toward* **DAD***)* I'm completely calm – I got the gun. Now, you go sit down.

*(**DAD** crosses to dining room and sits at the table.)*

VINNY. Hey Tony, you want me to close the door?

TONY. Shhhh! What'd I say you idiot?!

VINNY. You said… "go sit down."

TONY. No moron, before we came to the door?…

VINNY. …you said that we… "shouldn't call each other by name – so's they wouldn't be able to identify us." Right, Tony?

TONY. YA DID IT AGAIN!!!

VINNY. Sorry! Sorry…Wentworth – sorry.

TONY. "Wentworth"!?!? Look, you idiot–yous already spilled the beans on my name, so it's a little late for aliases. And do I look like a "Wentworth"!?

BETH. No, you're definitely a *Tony*. And for what it's worth – you just said, "Me an' *Vinny* ain't real interested in goin' to jail." So I'd say you screwed up too… Wentworth.

TONY. *(points gun at* **BETH***)* Is anybody talkin' to yous missy? What's a matter, cat got your tongue? Good, cause I ain't interested in any yammerin' right now.

(He turns to walk away.)

BETH. *(under her breath)* Ha, then you came to the wrong house!

TONY. *(spins around)* Excuse me!

BETH. I said I'll be as quiet as a mouse.

AUNT ROSE. Is that gun real?

TONY. No it's a water pistol – I do door-to-door ice sculptures as Christmas presents!

AUNT ROSE. Well isn't that something!

(**UNCLE LEO** *just shakes his head.*)

TONY. Great, of all the houses to hide out in – we had to choose the nut house.

BETH. You got that one right!

VINNY. It's better than gettin' busted by the cops.

AUNT ROSE. Are you two in some kinda trouble?

TONY. No ma'am, we always take hostages on Christmas Eve – it's a family tradition.

AUNT ROSE. (*looks at* **UNCLE LEO**) Well, that certainly is an odd tradition.

TONY. (*points gun at* **AUNT ROSE**) Lady, do you think yous could stop talking for a minute and lemme think?!

AUNT ROSE, Why certainly, sir. As a matter of fact –

UNCLE LEO. ROSE!

AUNT ROSE. Sorry, sir – I talk a lot when I get excited.

BETH. She stays excited.

TONY. EVERYBODY CLOSE YER MOUTHS!!!!

(**VINNY** *closes his mouth tightly and covers it with one hand.*)

Not you, moron – I'm talkin' ta dese people!

(*Waves gun around for emphasis. Everyone ducks to protect themselves except for* **AUNT ROSE.**)

UNCLE LEO. Rose get your head down!

AUNT ROSE. Why, Leo – it ain't real – he uses it to make ice sculptures. Wouldn't it be great to hire him for next year?!

DAD: Rose – he was being sarcastic. That's a very real pistol.

BETH. Not to be confused with *sorta* real pistols – the kind that are used to sorta kill people.

DAD. Beth, be quiet.

VINNY. Is he your dad?

BETH. Yes.

VINNY. A pretty girl like you'd do good ta listen to 'im. Tony can get a little riled up on account of his situation –

TONY. This ain't Oprah – so cease wit' th' conversatin'! For th' record – dis is a *real* pistol dat fires *real* bullets. So don't be getting' no stupid ideas about bein' a hero or nuttin.' Me an' Vinny, we don't wanna hurt nobody. We jus' need a place to hide out for a little while til th' cops get tired of lookin' for us–and then we'll be on our way.

UNCLE LEO. That's good – that's real good. We don't want any trouble either.

AUNT ROSE. Absolutely not.

TONY. Good.

AUNT ROSE. We don't want any trouble whatsoever.

TONY. Glad to hear it.

AUNT ROSE. Nosiree – we don't want any problems at all.

UNCLE LEO. That's enough, Rose.

AUNT ROSE. No trouble at all

UNCLE LEO. ROSE! Drop it!!

TONY. Okay, listen – what was everybody doin' before we came in?

BETH. Just waiting to slit our wrists...

DAD. Well...we were about to have Christmas Eve dinner.

TONY. If da cops show up – I want everything to look natural. Maybe we should go on wit' da dinner. You –

BUNNY. Me?

TONY. Yeah, you – what's ya name?

BUNNY. Bunny.

TONY. *(looking at* **BUD***)* Very funny and I suppose yer Daffy Duck?! What's yer real name, "Bunny"?

BUNNY. Hortense.

TONY. *(long pause)* ...Okay, Bunny it is.

VINNY. "Bunny". I kinda like that – you look like a "Bunny".

TONY. Thank you for yer insight, Vincent – now shut up. Bunny, yous go and get everything and put it on da table, and take the two girls wit' yas. Vinny, yous go keep an eye on 'em.

VINNY. No problem, Tony. *(starts to exit, then comes back to* **TONY***)* Um, what am I keepin' an eye on 'em for?

TONY. So's they don't try to escape or call da cops or nothin'- what are you, stupid or somethin??

VINNY. *(pause)* ...No.

TONY. Then go in da kitchen and make sure there ain't no monkey business goin' on.

*(***VINNY*** exits.)*

Alright, listen – I want everybody to get comfortable and look natural in case da cops come by. Sit down... sit.

(They all find a seat.)

Who's house is dis?

DAD. It's mine.

TONY. If the bell rings – yer gonna answer it.

DAD. Yes, sir.

TONY. And no funny business.

DAD. No – no funny business.

TONY. If I'm goin' ta jail – I may as well go for assault as for robbery if you catch my drift.

DAD. I understand.

TONY. Good, then I'm sure you won't have no problem tellin' da cops that we're all one, big, happy family.

AUNT ROSE. Thomas, is this Tony related to us?

DAD. No, Aunt Rose.

AUNT ROSE. You look a little like my cousin Arlene's side of the family.

TONY. There's no relation.

AUNT ROSE. Are you sure – you got the same eyes –

TONY. I'm sure, now could yous sit down and zip it.

AUNT ROSE. *(to* UNCLE LEO*)* He's rude enough to be a member of our family.

TONY. *(pacing, nervous)* This does not look natural. Whata yous people do when ya have these dinners?

BUD. Pretty much what we're doing right now. We all sit around looking bored while Rose talks non-stop, and Leo picks his fingernails.

*(*UNCLE LEO *looks up surprised and stops cleaning his nails.)*

TONY. Whata you do?

BUD. Me?

TONY. No, the lamp – yeah, you.

BUD. I dunno. I usually sit and pretend I'm listening.

TONY. Ta what?

BUD. To Rose's story.

TONY. Ta what story?

BUD. To the one she's usually telling as I'm sitting here.

TONY. This is perfect – just perfect. If da cops show up, then yer gonna sit there an' act like yer listenin' to a story, that ain't bein' told?!

BUD. Yeah, pretty much.

TONY. You'd better be convincin'. *(to* UNCLE LEO*)* Whata 'bout you old man?

UNCLE LEO. I never listen to her stories.

TONY. What?

UNCLE LEO. I've heard 'em all a hundred times – when she starts in on one, I daydream.

TONY. You daydream?!?!

UNCLE LEO. Every time.

TONY. *(pause)* About what?

UNCLE LEO. Marlene Dietrich.

TONY. Marlene Dietrich?

UNCLE LEO. Not "Mar-lene". "Mar-le-ne". She hated it when people called her "Mar-lene". Sent her into a tizzy.

AUNT ROSE. Oh, here he goes again on Marlene Dietrich. The woman's been dead for nearly twenty years – give up the ghost, Leo!

UNCLE LEO. You're just jealous.

AUNT ROSE. Jealous?! Jealous of what?!

UNCLE LEO. Of my relationship with Marlene.

AUNT ROSE. That's ridiculous! Besides, I thought you said you never had a "relationship" with her?!

UNCLE LEO. I didn't.

AUNT ROSE. Then how can I be jealous of a relationship you didn't have?!

TONY. Okay, that's enough.

UNCLE LEO. Because that's just like something you'd do.

AUNT ROSE. What's that supposed to mean?

UNCLE LEO. You know exactly what it means!

TONY. That's enough!

AUNT ROSE. May be if you hadn't spent your lunch break everyday chasin' skirts around Times Square –

UNCLE LEO. I was never unfaithful to you a day in my life –

TONY. *(screaming)* SHUT UP!!! That's enough! I don't wanna hear another word. *(crosses up center to dining room door)* Hey, Vinny – are yous guys killin' the hog yerselves?!

VINNY. *(appears through kitchen door)* Huh?

TONY. What is takin' so long in there?

VINNY. Oh, we was waitin' on the rolls to brown.

TONY: I don't care if we got rolls or not – get the food on th' table – these people are drivin' me nuts!!! *(crosses down right to area below sofa)* Alright look: we're all gonna go in the dinin' room and sit down and eat. And we ain't gonna be listenin' to stories that ain't bein' told. And we ain't gonna be daydreamin' about Marelene Dietrich. And we ain't gonna be accusin' nobody of nothin'. We're just gonna eat. Period. Am I clear?!

(They all nod.)

Good, now get up an' get in th' dinin' room.

(They exit up center.)

BUNNY. Okay, everybody find a seat. Tom, where do you want everyone?

DAD. Uh –

TONY. Never mind that – just sit down anywhere.

BUNNY. Well, we can't just sit anywhere.

TONY. Why not?

BUNNY. Well if the police show up and a teenage girl is seated at the head of the table – don't you think that'll look a little suspicious?

DAD. *(under his breath)* Stop being so *helpful,* Bunny.

TONY. Yeah, yeah – yer prob'ly right. You – Dad – sit at the head o' the table. Uncle Leo – you sit at th' other end.

BETH. *(snidely)* Do we get to sit at the "big person table"?

TONY. Are you bustin' my chops? Don't be bustin' my chops. Just get a chair and sit down. Hey Vinny…

(VINNY enters from the kitchen wearing an apron.)

What are yous doin?

VINNY. I'm gettin' the rolls.

TONY. Why yas wearin' an apron?

VINNY. I didn' wanna get nothin' on me.

BETH. What are those – your good robbery clothes?

TONY. You beat anything I ever seen.

VINNY. I'm jus' doin' what yous said to do – I'm lookin' like a member of the family. Isn't that what yous said?

TONY. Well yeah, but I didn' mean that yous was supposed to actually cook.

VINNY. I like cookin'.

TONY. Yer kiddin' me.

VINNY. No seriously, it's a lot less stressful than robbin' stores.

BETH. And a lot less frowned upon.

TONY. Just pass out those rolls and sit down.

VINNY. Sure thing. Would you like a roll? How 'bout yous? Careful they're still hot…

(TONY is getting agitated at VINNY's kindness.)

How 'bout you, lady – you want one?

(TONY reaches over and with his bare hands starts throwing rolls down on everyone's plates.)

TONY. Here – one for you, and you. And one for you, and you and you, and one for you!!!

VINNY. Ya know, Tony, with the swine flu goin' 'round – you really shoulda washed your hands before yas touched everybody's roll.

TONY. Would you sit down!!!

VINNY. Geez, somebody gets testy when he hasn' eaten.

TONY. Don't you go bustin' my chops neither – I got a lot on my mind.

BETH. Worried about the performance of your portfolio in this fragile economic down-turn – or just stressed about where you're gonna find soap-on-a-rope at six thirty on Christmas Eve?

TONY. Listen smarty-pants, when I want your comments – I'll rattle yer cage.

BETH. Ooooo, "smarty-pants" – that's mighty strong talk for such a savvy criminal like yourself.

DAD. Beth – that's enough.

TONY. Daddy's right, Beth – that's enough – now shut it.

AUNT ROSE. What kind of Christmas Eve dinner is this? There's no meat??

BUNNY. *(startled, hops up from her seat)* Oh my goodness gracious – I was in such a hurry – *(taps TONY on the head with a serving spoon)* 'cause somebody was rushin' me – I totally forgot to get it.

VINNY. What is it? – I'll get it.

TRACY. Ham – its in the oven.

VINNY. Ham?! – No way, I ain't touchin' it.

TRACY. Why not?

VINNY. I'm a vegetarian – I don't eat the stuff.

BETH. You're a vegetarian?!

VINNY. Mostly – I still eat egg McMuffins – minus the Canadian bacon of course.

BETH. For how long?

VINNY. How long have I been eatin' egg McMuffins?

BETH. No, how long have you been a vegetarian?

VINNY. About six months. I read this article in *Reader's Digest* and thought I'd give it a try. Do you have any idea what they put in all those processed meats?!

BETH. Oh, I know – it's disgusting what people will ingest.

VINNY. It's pretty disgusting what they'll *eat* too.

TONY. Hey, Bobby Flay – if you're done tradin' recipes – the rest of us'd like to have some o' dat ham.

VINNY. It's all you, dude – I told yas – I ain't touchin' it.

(*BUNNY enters from kitchen carrying the ham on a platter.*)

BUNNY. Here we goooo.

BETH. Disgusting.

BUD. Looks great to me – how 'bout you Leo?

UNCLE LEO. I'll try it, but I'm telling ya – if it didn't come from Schnellendahl's don't expect much.

BUNNY. It'll be wonderful because Janet bought it, and she always gets the best.

UNCLE LEO. Did it come from Schnellendahl's?

BUNNY. I doubt it.

UNCLE LEO. Then she didn't get the best.

BUNNY. You don't know that. When's the last time you bought a ham from anybody other than Schnellendahl's?

UNCLE LEO. I would *never* buy a ham anywhere else. Ever.

BUNNY. So then you really don't have a point of reference.

UNCLE LEO. Whata ya mean by that?!

BUNNY. If the only ham you've ever had came from one place – then you have nothing to compare it to.

UNCLE LEO. You don't know what your talkin' 'bout!

TONY. Shut up.

BUNNY. And you do, Mr. "I only get ham from one place"?

TONY. I said shut up.

UNCLE LEO. You wouldn't know a good ham if it bit you in the butt –

TONY. SHUT UP!! Nobody cares about the ham!! Just eat it!

(There is an awkward silence as the platter is passed around the table.)

DAD. Alright…well…let's just pass everything around to the left. Here ya go…

BUD. Thank you.

TONY. Vinny, go look out th' front window, and see if th' cops are goin' door to door yet.

VINNY. Yeah sure thing. *(to BETH)* Uh, do you think you could make me a plate – just give me the same stuff you like –

TONY. Stop fraternizin' with th' enemy and get in th' livin' room!

VINNY. Make him a plate too – maybe he'll stop bein' so testy.

TONY. GO!!

BETH. What do you want on your plate, Wentworth?

TONY. Very funny.

BETH. Who's kidding? – What do you want??

TONY. I'm not hungry.

BETH. Suit yourself.

DAD. Well, this isn't exactly what Janet and I had planned, but we're glad you're all here…most of you any way.

TONY. This ain't exactly what we had planned either.

BETH. *(to DAD)* Are you going to say grace?

DAD. Yes…I am. Let's bow our heads. Dear Heavenly Father, thank you for this time that we have as family and thank you for the many blessings that you've given us. Please watch over Janet as she travels and bring her safely back to us. It's in your name that we pray… Amen. Uh…where's a knife to carve the ham?

TONY, Whoa, whoa – nobody's getting' a knife. What you think we are – idiots?!

BETH. Pretty much.

DAD. Beth, be quiet. No we don't think that at all. But if we're going to eat the ham we have to be able to cut it.

VINNY. My dad would always cut ours with an electric knife. I used to love the sound of it.

(He makes a buzzing noise as if he were using an electric knife, then **TONY** *hits him on the back of the head.)*

TONY. That's the first smart thing yous said all day. *(looks at* **DAD***)* You got an electric knife?

DAD. Yeah – in the kitchen.

TONY. Good, go get it.

*(***DAD** *exits to kitchen.)*

BUNNY. Who needs butter for their roll? Tracy?

TRACY. Yes ma'am, thanks. Here come the green beans.

(She picks up the bowl and passes it around the table. **DAD** *enters with the electric knife. He plugs it in and sits down.)*

BUD. Do you need a hand?

DAD. Thanks, but I think I've got it.

(He turns on the knife and begins to cut the ham.)

Tell ya what, Bud, as I slice it – why don't you stack it on the platter.

BUD. You got it.

(He starts stacking the ham on the platter.)

Pass me your plate and I'll put some meat on there for ya. Rose, Leo, pass yer plates.

UNCLE LEO. God must've blessed this ham – because it's alright.

AUNT ROSE. Leo, stop bein' persnickety.

UNCLE LEO. Who's bein' persnickety?! I said I like it.

AUNT ROSE. You said it's "alright." That's not the same as sayin' you like it.

TONY. Do you two always act like this?! You can't even agree when you're agreein'!

UNCLE LEO. Who's agreein'? I just said it was good.

AUNT ROSE. You did not – you said it was alright –

TONY: Okay that's it – SHUT. UP.

(**VINNY** *appears in doorway.*)

VINNY. Hey, Tony – is my plate ready? – I'm hungry.

TONY. For the love of Christmas – get out there and make sure that the cops don't bust us.

BETH. You need to eat.

TONY. You need to mind your own business.

BETH. Mind my own business?!? I was minding my own business – *you're* the one that barged into *my house!*

TONY. Biggest mistake I've made in a long time!

BETH. Yeah, well any time you wanna reverse your fortunes, you can move on, and we'll all be just fine.

TONY. What, so yous can call th' cops and get us sent ta jail?! I think I'll pass on that.

(**BETH** *picks up pate and moves toward door.*)

Where do you think yer goin?

BETH. To give Vinny his dinner.

(**TONY** *pulls out the gun and points it at her.*)

What – you going to shoot me over some green beans and a pile of mashed potatoes?

TONY. Don't try anything stupid.

BETH. No problem – that's your category.

(*She exits to living room.*)

BUNNY. *(trying to lighten the mood)* Has everyone been good this year so Santa's sure to bring you something nice?!

(*They all look at her with a blank stare, irritated.*)

BUD. Just eat.

BUNNY. I was just trying to introduce a little of the Christmas spirit, but obviously I'm in a room full o' Grinches.

(The lights fade to black on the dining room as they come up on **VINNY** *and* **BETH** *in the living room.)*

BETH. Here. *(hands him his plate)*

VINNY. Thanks...why you bein' so nice.

BETH. Do I have a choice – you've got guns.

VINNY. I get yer point...thanks.

(takes the plate and begins to eat as **BETH** *walks away)*

BETH. Hey Vinny...

VINNY. Yeah?...

BETH. ...never mind.

(She exits into the dining room as the lights cross fade.)

TONY. *(mocking)* You and "veggie boy" have a good little chat?

BETH. Shut up. *(She crosses to chair and sits.)*

TONY. Now dis is th' way I like it – good and quiet.

AUNT ROSE. Oh, not me! Is there anything more boring on the entire planet that a family that sits around at dinner and don't say a single word?! Am I right, Leo?

UNCLE LEO. I wouldn't know – in fifty two years of marriage I never had that experience.

AUNT ROSE. Sure ya did – you're just so old ya prob'ly forgot it!

TONY. Oh no,no,no – you two are not starting again.

DAD. Does anyone need anything? Tracy, do you have enough?

TRACY. Yes, sir, I'm good thank you.

DAD. Beth, how 'bout you?

BETH. I'm fine, but I just remembered – I didn't get Vinny anything to drink.

TONY. Gimme a break – what are yous – his mother?!

BETH. What do you want?

TONY. I want yous to sit down and shut up.

BETH. I mean what do you want *to drink?!*

TONY. *(caught off-guard)* I'll have a Dr. Pepper – in a can. I don't want no funny business.

BETH. *(sarcastically)* Right, because everyone knows that in the kitchen... we keep knock-out drops under the sink. Sooo that on those occasions when we're having a family dinner in which WE'RE ALL TAKEN HOSTAGE – we'll be able to drug our captors, call the police, and make the front page of *The Times!* You've got us figured out! You are way too smart for us Tony– waaay too smart!! *(She exits to kitchen.)*

TONY. *(to* **DAD***)* How long til she leaves for college?

DAD. About eight months.

TONY. When she's gone – change the locks. Or better yet– move, and don't leave a forwarding address.

BUNNY. Tracy leaves in eight months too – she and Beth are the same age you know. They're both gonna be Valedictorians of their class. Aren't you dear?

TRACY. I don't know...I guess.

BUNNY. She's just bein' modest – she's a little shy like that. Were you ever a valedictorian?

(Everyone looks at her in disbelief.)

TONY. ...yeah...and a Rhodes Scholar too. I was a regular Albert Einstein – whata you, crazy!?!

(Suddenly, the doorbell rings.)

QUIET–Nobody moves!

(He crosses to door, whispers to **VINNY***.)*

Who is it?

VINNY. I can't tell – it's some man in blue –

TONY. IT'S THE COPS – DON'T ANYBODY MAKE A SOUND!!!

(Lights fade quickly to black as the curtain closes.)

END OF ACT ONE.

ACT TWO

Scene One: The Man in Blue

(As the scene opens, we pick up where Act One left off. **TONY** *and* **VINNY** *are crouched below the bay window trying to see who is at the door, but are unable to make out the person.)*

*(***TONY*** *crosses to the dining room and gets* **DAD***.)*

TONY. Alright, Mister: I want you to open the door – and no funny business. I'd hate to hafta hurt anybody...

DAD. That won't be necessary.

(He opens the door and we see a teenage boy standing there with blue hair and dressed in gothic style clothing. It is their neighbor, **PAUL WAKOWSKI***.)*

PAUL. Hey Mr. Douglas, uh, Merry Christmas.

DAD. Merry Christmas, Paul.

PAUL. My mom wanted me to drop off this gift for you... and I was hoping that I could maybe give this to Beth?

(He has a gift for her in his hand.)

DAD. Well, actually...

TONY. Get rid of him.

DAD. ...she's gone out for a few minutes...

PAUL. In a snowstorm?

DAD. She had some last minute shopping to do.

PAUL. Her car's still parked in the driveway.

DAD. Well...uh...

TONY. *(from behind door)* Alright, get him in here – now!

DAD. Why don't you come in out of the snow?

41

(PAUL *enters and when* DAD *closes the door he sees* TONY *standing there holding the gun. Instinctively, he puts his hands up.*)

PAUL. Whoa – don't shoot.

TONY. Just get away from the window.

PAUL. Mr. Douglas, what's going on?

DAD. It's a long story.

TONY. Look, kid – we're just hidin' out here for a few minutes til the cops leave the area, and then we're outta here. You stay calm and everything'll turn out fine. Now get in th' dining room.

(*They cross to dining room door and enter.*)

VINNY. Boy, that was close.

TONY. I thought you said he was "a man in blue?!"

VINNY. Well, his *hair* was blue…

TONY. That ain't th' same, Vinny – I thought he was a cop!

VINNY. He's kinda young to be a cop, don't ya think?

TONY. – well of course he's – oh forget it, I don't have the energy to explain it. You about gave me a heart attack!

VINNY. Man, am I glad you didn't do that. My CPR certification ran out six months ago.

TONY. You had CPR trainin'?

VINNY. Oh yeah, I used ta be a lifeguard at the Y.

TONY. The YMCA?

VINNY. Yeah, it was cool. The job I mean – but don't get no ideas or nothin'. It really ain't that fun (*starts to sing and do hand motions*) "ta stay at th' Y.M.C.A."

TONY. Yer an idiot – get in th' dinin' room.

(*They both exit to dining room.*)

VINNY. It's gettin' kinda crowded in here, Tony.

TONY. (*clearly agitated at having another hostage*) I can see that – I'm not blind.

BETH. Which is too bad – 'cause you'd look so cute with one of those little, white, canes.

TONY. Shut up – I'm thinkin'!

BETH. *(to TRACY)* I thought I smelled smoke.

TONY. Alright, here's what we're doin': I want all yous ladies in th' livin' room. All the men are stayin' here in th' dinin' room.

BUD. You mean we don't get seconds?

TONY. We're not runnin' a restaurant here – dis is a hostage situation! Ladies, get in th' livin' room.

BUNNY. Oh no sir, we can't go in th' livin' room. We haven't had dessert yet.

TONY. What??!!??

BUNNY. I worked very hard on that, and we're not gonna go without eating it!

TONY. You gotta be kiddin' me, lady?!

BUD. You haven't lived, til you've had one o' her cakes.

VINNY. What kind is it?

TONY. Would you shut up?!

VINNY. *(to TONY)* I'm still hungry – *(to BUNNY)* what kind is it?

BUNNY. My famous carrot cake.

TONY. Naturally…it's only fittin' that "Bunny" would bring a carrot cake. You people are whacked!

VINNY. Carrot cake's my favorite – cut me a big piece –

UNCLE LEO. Me too – that sounds good –

TONY. ALRIGHT, FINE! Yous can all have cake. BUT, the men are stayin' in dis room and the ladies is eatin' in th –

BETH. –are eating.

TONY. What?!

BETH. "Are" eating. You said: "Ladies is." The "ladies *is* eating." It's actually, "The ladies *are* eating." That's correct English.

TONY. Excuuuse me, Daniel Webster! "The ladies *are* eatin' their cake in the livin' room!!

BETH. Dad's gonna flip.

TONY. What?!?

BETH. Dad's really particular about the Victorian couch. It's over a hundred years old and he hardly lets us sit on it –

DAD: Beth –

BETH. It's the truth. You freak whenever I get near it. *(to* **TONY***)* There's no way he's gonna let us eat on it.

TONY. And why not?

BETH. Someone could get icing on it.

TONY. *(holds up the pistol)* And just how would he feel about blood on it?…

DAD. It's no problem, really…

TONY. See, that was easy. Now get yer cake and get in th' other room.

BUNNY. I need dessert plates and a cake knife.

TONY. I already got yous a knife!

BUNNY. That's an electric knife – it's for meat. You can't cut *cake* with a meat knife. Well, I guess you *could*, but it'd probably fly all over the place.

TONY. Oh, for the love o' Christmas – fine – Vinny, yer th' cake lover – get th' lady a *cake knife. (to* **BETH***)* You – go get dessert plates. *(to* **TRACY***)* You – go with her.

(They exit.)

AUNT ROSE. I really don't want to be a bother –

BUD. *(under his breath)* Too late for that…

AUNT ROSE. – but dessert is hardly dessert without coffee. Thomas, do you have any coffee?

DAD. There's none made, but –

TONY. ABSOLUTELY NOT! Do you peoples not see what's goin' on here?! You. Are. Being. Held. Hostage!! This ain't Starbucks!

UNCLE LEO. Praise th' Lord. Worst coffee in the world. Dishwater – that's all you get at Starbucks – dishwater.

AUNT ROSE. Leo –

[handwritten marginalia: "Blood on the couch" / "Bunny's knife" / "Leslik" / "CLASSIC ROSE"]

UNCLE LEO. Now, that Jewish coffee shop in mid-town – *(to* **AUNT ROSE***)* what's it called?

AUNT ROSE. *He Brews?*

UNCLE LEO. *He Brews* – now that's a real cup o' coffee!

BUD. "He Brews?" That's pretty funny. I never heard o' that one. I prefer *Java The Hut.*

UNCLE LEO. Does George Lucas own that one?

BUD. I wouldn't doubt it.

UNCLE LEO. That's another man that's a genius! Turned a bunch of goofy space creatures into a trillion dollar industry. The man's brilliant I'm tellin' ya.

AUNT ROSE. The subject is coffee Leo – no one cares about George Lucas. My new favorite is that international coffee shop in Greenwich: *Bean Around The World.*

BUNNY. Oh, we don't have that one in Trenton, but for my money it's hard to beat a good cup from *Brewed Awakenings.*

DAD. "Brewed awakenings?!" Oh, that's good. I think my choice would have to be the little coffee house that this church down the street runs.

UNCLE LEO. Is it good?

DAD. Uh the coffee's not bad, but the name is great: *Sacred Grounds.*

BUD. Now that's a funny name.

DAD. Paul do you drink coffee?

PAUL. Yeah, but I don't go ta any o' those places.

BUNNY. Where do young people like yourself go these days?

PAUL. There's this science fiction themed coffee shop that we hang at – it's called *Bean Me Up.*

TONY. *(exasperated)* Yous guys should get yer own talk show! Or better yet – don't! Hey you – blueberry.

PAUL. Me?

TONY. *(sarcastically)* No, th' other one wit' blue hair.

UNCLE LEO. Rose?

TONY. No, him, you idiot! *(points at* **PAUL***)* You make coffee?

PAUL. Yeah, I make coffee.

TONY. Get in th' kitchen and make some. All dis coffee talk's done got me wantin' a cup.

AUNT ROSE. *Coffee Talk* that would be a good name.

BUNNY. Isn't funny how we –

TONY. *(interrupts rudely)* No, it's not funny! Shut up.

(She smiles, unfazed. The kitchen door opens and the girls enter carrying the cake. **VINNY** *is about to sit down)*

Whoa, what are you doin'?

VINNY. 'm sittin' down ta eat my cake.

TONY. No yer not.

VINNY. I'm not?

TONY. No, yer goin' in th' kitchen wit' th' Smurf here and makin' coffee.

VINNY. I dunno how ta make coffee – I just drink it.

TONY. Well, lucky for you then that he came over.

(Waves him off. **PAUL** *and* **VINNY** *exit into the kitchen. The girls begin handing out cake to everyone.)*

BUD. Now that's what I'm talkin' about.

TONY. It's what *everybody's* talkin' about. That's all yous guys do is talk.

(The doorbell rings. **TONY** *tenses up.)*

Alright, people – everybody shut yer mouths and don't move. *(crosses to kitchen door)* Vinny – get out here!

VINNY. What?

TONY. It's the doorbell.

VINNY. I don't fix those either.

TONY. No, dim-wit! Somebody rang the doorbell.

VINNY. Who?

TONY. I dunno who – that's the problem. What if it's th' cops?!

VINNY. Then we are totally up a creek.

TONY. Well, I certainly ain't goin' ta jail on account o' these morons. *(to **DAD**)* C'mon. We're goin' ta see who's at th' door. *(to **VINNY**)* Keep an eye on 'em – and don't take no monkey business if ya know what I mean.

*(**TONY** and **DAD** exit to living room as lights dim in dining room.)*

Don't go thinkin' 'bout nothin' cute – I'd hate ta hafta shoot yous. Now, look out th' peep hole. Who is it?

DAD. It's Emily.

TONY. What am I – yer social planner? Who's that?!

DAD. She's a neighbor girl.

TONY. Alright…open th' door an' invite hers in.

DAD. I can probably get rid of her.

TONY. Nice try – get her in here!

*(**DAD** opens the door.)*

DAD. Hello, Emily.

EMILY. Hi, Mr. Douglas. Have you seen Paul?

DAD. Yes…yes I have. Would you like to come in?

*(She enters and **TONY** steps from behind the door.)*

EMILY. Yes sir, it's freezing out here.

TONY. Welcome to th' party.

EMILY. Is that a gun?

TONY. Oh for th' love o' Pete – we're not goin' through dis again! YES, it's a gun. A *real* gun, that I will use to shoot you if you start talkin'. I've had enough talkin' for one night!

DAD. It's okay, Emily, he's not going to hurt us – he's just here for a while and then he'll be gone. Right, Tony?

TONY. Dats th' plan. Keep yer mouth shut, don't try nuthin' stupid – and everything'll be fine.

(They cross to the dining room and the lights restore.)

VINNY. Another one!

TONY. They're multiplyin' like rabbits 'round here.

VINNY. If anymore people show up – we're gonna need a bigger house.

PAUL. What are you doing here?

EMILY. Mom sent me to find *you.*

PAUL. Why?

EMILY. You've been gone for fifteen minutes. How long could it take to drop off one little present?

VINNY. It's was actually two presents.

EMILY. Two?

VINNY. Yeah, the one your mom sent, and the one he brought for Beth.

EMILY. You brought Beth a present?   **BETH.** You brought me a present?

PAUL. *(embarrassed)* Well, uh…

BUNNY. *(to BUD)* Isn't that sweet?!

VINNY. Why don't you open it?

BETH. *(awkward)* Well, I…

TONY. *(to VINNY)* Have you lost your mind!?! We are not playin' "dirty Santa" here –

BUNNY. Bud played Dirty Santy once and –

TRACY. Mother, gross!

TONY. *(to the group)* Look, I put up wit' yer slicin' ham and servin' cake and I was even fine wit' makin' coffee, but I draw the line at openin' presents. There will be NO present opening.

VINNY. *(pauses)* …were you neglected as a child?…

(Lights quick fade to black. End of scene.)

Scene Two: Family Ties

(When the lights come up, it is a short while later. The action of this scene alternates between the two rooms. The lights will intensify in the room in which we see the action. At curtain, the lights are up in the dining room.)

BUNNY. *(sheepishly)* Mr. Tony?...

TONY. What.

BUNNY. ...can I make a suggestion?

TONY. Why do I get th' feelin' dat no matter what I say – you're gonna do it anyway?

BUNNY. Oh, thank you. Um, well...I know that you want to split us up – and I must admit that it is getting quite crowded in here. But...well, frankly I think that the *men* should go to the *living room* and the *women* should stay in the *dining room.*

TONY. Naturally, because you people live in "opposite world" where you all have your own separate reality. But, please – I'm dyin' ta know: why do yous think dat?

BUNNY. Oh there are lots of reasons.

TONY. Enlighten me.

BUNNY: First of all: if we leave, the men will sit here and eat this entire ham and then when my sister gets here –

TONY. You mean there are *more people* coming?!?

BUNNY. Well of course, she lives here!

TONY. Of course – what was I thinkin'?

BUNNY. Well anyway, like I was sayin': there won't be any ham left when she gets here. And these guys are all wonderful–don't get me wrong, but all these dirty dishes would crawl on their own to the dishwasher, before a single one of them would even think for one minute to actually clear the table.

TONY. Yous wanna stay here so you can clean the dining room?

(She nods and smiles. He shakes his head in disbelief.)

TONY. *(cont.)* Far be it from me ta stand in th' way o' tidiness. Men: get in th' livin' room.

(They all grumble and then begin to exit. **BUD** *reaches across the table and picks up a large piece of ham and walks out with it.)*

Vinny, yous supervise th' clean up and pay attention.

VINNY. No problem, Tony.

*(***TONY*** *exits to living room.)*

TONY. Dis is more like it. Niiiiice and quiet.

UNCLE LEO. Segregation of the sexes – we shoulda thought o' this a long time ago.

BUD: I *did* think of it a long time ago. Bunny sits in the sun room and talks on the phone, while I lay around in the den and watch bowling

DAD. You watch *bowling?*

BUD. Yeah…is there something wrong with that?

DAD. *(hesitant)* …no…I guess not…

UNCLE LEO. Yes, there is something wrong with that. It's *bowling!!* The only thing more boring that *playing* bowling is *watching* bowling.

BUD. You don't *play* bowling. You "bowl".

UNCLE LEO. No, I don't – 'cause it sucks.

BUD. You're crazy.

UNCLE LEO. I'm not crazy – you're the one watching it. There's no drama – they're too good. *(sarcastic)* "Oh look, he got a strike – I wonder how this guy'll do? – Another strike – amazing!! Oh my goodness – he only got nine pins, I wonder if he'll pick up the spare?!?!" There's no drama, I'm tellin' ya.

BUD. *(clearly irritated)* Excuuuse me, Leo – sorry that I lead such a dull life. I'll try to jazz it up a little this week. Maybe I'll have coffee at *He Brews* and then stop by *Schnellendahl's* and pick up a ham on my way over to visit Irving Berlin –

TONY. YOU ARE RUININ' MY QUIET PLACE!

(They stop arguing, **TONY** *pauses and speaks calmly.)*

Sit there and don't say nuthin'. Nuthin'. Yer worse dan th' women!

(The lights fade quickly on the living room and come up on the dining room.)

AUNT ROSE. Do you know what I'm sayin'?

BETH. *(under her breath)* We haven't got a clue…

TRACY. Mom, are you worried?

BUNNY. About what?

TRACY. MOM! We are being held *hostage!!*

BUNNY. Oh, that.

TRACY. Yes, *that.*

BUNNY. Listen girls…there's nothing to be worried about. If the Police come – there will be a long standoff and a lot of negotiations, and they'll send us some pizza.

BETH. Pizza?

BUNNY. It's what they always do – then they'll either talk Tony into doing the smart thing and surrendering, or–

TRACY. Or what?

BUNNY. They'll fire tear gas through the windows, kick in the doors, and shoot them both on the spot. Hopefully not injuring any hostages in the process!

EMILY. And you know all this, how?

BUNNY. Oh, I watch *Law and Order.*

EMILY. You watch *Law and Order…*

BUNNY. It's how they always handle it on the police shows.

VINNY. You think they're gonna shoot us – seriously?!

AUNT ROSE. Well, it stands to reason –

BUNNY. Noooo, they're not gonna shoot you silly! Tony will wise up and do the right thing. And then you'll both go to prison.

VINNY. Prison?!?

AUNT ROSE. *Federal* Prison.

VINNY. What if he doesn't wise up?

BETH. Best case scenario?

VINNY. Yeah.

BETH. They bust down the door, hit you with a tazer, and you pee yourself –

VINNY. Pee Myself!

BETH. Then you crumple to the floor in the fetal position while sucking your thumb.

VINNY. I don't like th' sound o' any o' doze. Idn't there another option?

AUNT ROSE. Well, I suppose the police might stop looking for you and move on.

EMILY. Or they might not be looking for you in this area at all.

BUNNY. In which case you two can just be on your merry way. No pun intended.

BETH. HA! – Fat chance.

(The lights fade down quickly on the dining room and come up on the living room. **BUD** *has all the candy from the dish poured out on the table and is digging through it.)*

BUD. Are there any more chocolate snow men?

TONY. What are yous – a garbage disposal?! Ya been eatin' since I got here.

BUD. I got a fast metabolism.

UNCLE LEO. Especially when the food's free.

BUD. Besides your constant sarcasm and stunning wit – what exactly did *you* bring for the meal Leo, huh?

DAD. Fellas, that's enough. We're family here.

PAUL. You guys are all related?

UNCLE LEO. Unfortunately.

PAUL. How?

DAD. Tracy is the daughter of Bud and Bunny. My wife Janet, is Bunny's sister, which makes Bud and I brother-in-laws.

UNCLE LEO. "Brothers-in-law."

BUD. What are you – an English major?!

UNCLE LEO. As a matter of fact: yes.

BUD. And you think *bowling* is boring?!

DAD. *(cutting them off)* Rose is my wife's Aunt and Leo here is her husband.

UNCLE LEO. It just goes to show: you can pick ya friends, but buddy you're stuck with ya relatives.

(The lights fade quickly on the living room and come up on the dining room.)

BETH. I knew there was always something nauseating about Mom and Dad...

BUNNY. Oh no, it was very sweet. Your father was quite a romantic.

TRACY. What about you, Mom – how did you and Dad meet?

BUNNY. Well, it's kind of a long story.

VINNY. *(very interested)* It's not like we're goin' anywhere.

(They turn and look at him momentarily.)

BUNNY. Well, if you really want to hear it...

*(They all look interested except **BETH**.)*

It was the early 80's and I was workin' as a waitress at "The Buck and Bass Inn" on Lake Owassa – in northern Jersey. One weekend they were havin' a fishin' tournament at a neighborin' lake and we were slammed with fisherman comin' in for dinner.

TRACY. Was Dad fishing in the tournament?

BUNNY. Oh yes – and he was in fourth place at the time so he was pretty cocky that night I met him.

TRACY. Did you like him instantly?

BUNNY. Not at all – he was rude and he smelled like fish.

BETH. *(to herself)* That's the Bud we all know and love.

BUNNY. But when he walked into the restaurant, it was like something out of a Bon Jovi video. It all looked like slow motion as he waltzed in wearing a sleeveless T-shirt, with his boots clicking on the floor and his mullet blowing in the breeze.

BETH. It was probably the air passing through his ears.

BUNNY. I thought he was the cutest thing I'd ever seen.

BETH. *(quietly to* **EMILY***)* Emphasis on "*thing*".

BUNNY. The hostess sat him in another girl's section, but I paid her ten dollars to let me wait on him – which got me in a lot of trouble with other customers that couldn't understand why I'd walk right by them and not offer to take their orders.

AUNT ROSE. Goodness, that's half the places I've ever eaten. I wouldn't have thought a thing about it.

BUNNY. They were pretty miffed, but that's not really relevant to th' story. I went to the table and asked Bud what I could get him, and in the coyest voice I'd ever heard, he said: "That depends – are *you* on the menu?" I could've melted right there.

TRACY. What did you say?

BUNNY. I said: "If I was – you couldn't afford me with fourth place winnings" – I had ta put him in his place. *(The girls laugh.)* Then he says: "Well supposin' I win this thing?…" I didn't wanna seem too eager so I said: "Well, *if* you win it, *then* you can give me a call" – and I wrote my name and number on his forearm.

EMILY. You wrote it on his arm?

BUNNY. I was afraid he'd lose it if I put it on paper – he didn't look like the organized type. Besides, I knew he was gonna call whether he won or not.

EMILY. Since you're married – I'm assuming he called?

BUNNY. Actually, not right away.

TRACY. Why not?

AUNT ROSE. This is my favorite part of the story – it's typical Bud!

BUNNY. *(giggling)* Well, on the final day of the tournament, he hooked a big bass and as he was leanin' over the' side of th' boat to net him – when he lost his balance and fell and his whole upper body went into th' lake. The water washed my number off his arm and he was too embarrassed to come and ask me out.

(BUD'S BIG MISTAKE) FLANIER

$10 hook-up

BETH. Well, then how did you two hook up? Ew, that was a really bad pun – sorry.

AUNT ROSE. Go on – tell 'em.

BUNNY. That whole next evening, I kept checking the door. I was nervous as a cat. But Bud never came to the restaurant. I'd never been so disappointed in my life. Then I started thinking maybe he's not as bold as I imagined and he thought I was serious about th' whole finishing first thing. Finally, at closing time, I cashed out and split my tips with the bus boy and headed for home. When I got to my car – it was on empty, so I stopped at a local gas station – and there he was! I thought I was gonna pee my pants!!

(margin note, handwritten) disappointment

BETH. Like Aunt Rose does now.

BUNNY. So, I walked across the parking lot and said: "I guess you didn't win – is that why you didn't call?" He said: "No, I didn't win – but I was gonna call anyway." So I said: "Then why didn't ya?" "Well there's two reasons," he said. "First of all, I fell in the lake and your number washed off my arm – so I couldn't call. Besides, didn't you give me your *home* number?" "Yeah," I said. "Well how am I supposed to have called ya at home if ya haven't been home yet?" It was right then and there that I decided there was something special about this man – he was a genius!

(margin note, handwritten) Redneck love

BETH. *(to herself)* Over-statement.

AUNT ROSE. I think that's the greatest redneck love story I've ever heard.

VINNY. *(sniffling, wiping a tear)* Me too.

*(The lights fade down on the dining room and come up once again on the living room where we see **TONY** standing by the window as the others are still seated in their usual spots.)*

BUD. Hey Tony, can we cut on the T.V.?

TONY. Yer kiddin' me right?

BUD. Uh…no.

TONY. NO!

BUD. This is pretty boring.

TONY. *(pulls out the pistol)* Do you want me ta liven things up a little? – I mean I could shoot yous if ya think that'd help.

BUD. I'm really not that bored yet.

UNCLE LEO. I am – shoot him.

TONY. You guys are like a couple o' five year-olds – my two little boys get along better dan yous two. Shut up – or I'm gonna shoot yous both!

BUD. Can he be first so I can watch?

TONY. SHUT UP!!!

*(Suddenly **TONY** is distracted by something he sees out the bay window. He crouches down slightly and moves to the edge of the window to see out. He talks to himself.)*

Oh, you gotta be kiddin' me…

BUD. Actually no, I'd –

TONY. *(points gun directly at **BUD**)* I said, shut up. *(to **DAD**)* C'mere.

*(**DAD** gets up and crosses to window.)*

Whoa, not so close…Look out there…whata yous see?

DAD. A lot of snow. Wow, it's still slowly putting it down.

TONY. No, moron, who's that coming up your driveway?

*(**DAD** looks out window again squinting without his glasses.)*

DAD. Oh, that's Mrs. Wakowski.

TONY. Who's that?

DAD. It's Paul and Emily's mom.

TONY. Perfect – just perfect. That's exactly what we need – another hostage.

DAD. We could turn out the lights and pretend we're not home.

TONY. Very funny. Dontcha think she'd notice the lights goin' out as she walks up to th' door?!

DAD. I didn't think of that.

TONY. Whata yous take me for, an idiot? Sure yous did. 'Cause you know that if ya don't answer th' door – she'll call the cops. Answer the door, be polite and get her in here.

(The doorbell rings and **DAD** *opens the door.)*

DAD. Hello Mrs. Wakowski, won't you come in.

MRS. WAKOWSKI. I can't stay, I was just wondering if you'd seen – *(She spots* **PAUL** *across the room.)* Where have you been?!

PAUL. Isn't it obvious?

MRS. WAKOWSKI. Don't get smart with me – I'll strangle you til your face is the same color as your hair. Why didn't you drop off the gift and come straight back like I asked.

DAD. Mrs. Wak –

MRS. WAKOWSKI. I'll handle this!

PAUL. Mom.

MRS. WAKOWSKI. What?!

PAUL. I'd like you to meet Tony.

MRS. WAKOWSKI. *(turns, barely paying attention)* Pleasure. Now, would you mind explaining to me why you're still here? I was worried sick!

TONY. What Sid Vicious here is tryin' ta tell yous is that he is being held hostage.

MRS. WAKOWSKI. What?

TONY. *(pulls out pistol)* And so are you.

MRS. WAKOWSKI. Oh my goodness –

DAD. Calm down – he's not going to hurt anyone as long as we cooperate.

MRS. WAKOWSKI. *(runs across to* **PAUL***)* Oh, baby are you okay?!

PAUL. I'm fine, Mom.

MRS. WAKOWSKI. Are you sure.

PAUL. Yes. Actually, this is one of the cooler Christmas Eves that I can remember.

MRS. WAKOWSKI. Paul!

PAUL. I'm serious. Who else can say that they've been held hostage on Christmas Eve?

TONY. You, and sixty-three other people in dis house.

(Lights fade quickly to black. End of Scene Two.)

Scene Three: Exchanging Gifts

(As the lights come up, we see an even more agitated **TONY** *pacing across the living room floor. Finally, he crosses to the dining room door.)*

TONY. Vinny.

VINNY. Yeah?

TONY. It's awfully quiet – is there anything goin' on in there?

VINNY. No. It's quiet 'cause yous blew yer top and said that you'd punch the next person that spoke.

TONY. ...Yeah, well...I'm a little stressed.

VINNY. Really? – I didn't notice.

TONY. Why don't you stop bein' a comedian and go look out th' back door – make sure there ain't no cops prowlin' around.

VINNY. Sure thing.

(He exits into kitchen.)

AUNT ROSE. Excuse me.

TONY. What?

AUNT ROSE. I may be old, but I'm not in *Depends*. I need a bathroom break.

TRACY. I have to go too.

EMILY. So do I.

BUNNY. I wasn't going to say anything, but –

TONY. Alright already – geez Louise, you gals are pushy!

BETH. *(snidely)* You wait much longer and they're gonna be "sqooshy."

TONY. Is there a window in yer bathroom?

BETH. Yeah.

TONY. *(to **AUNT ROSE**)* Sorry lady – you ain't goin'.

AUNT ROSE. It's a tiny window, eight feet above the ground, and I'm eighty-three years old – I'd break a hip!

TONY. *(hesitates)* Alright fine – go, but if I hear one little sound that's out o' order – I'm comin' in there.

BETH. You're goin' to stand by the door and listen?

MRS. WAKOWSKI. That's sick.

TONY. Just go pee!!!

> *(The lights fade down on the dining room as AUNT ROSE exits into the hall. They come up on the living room where we see the men seated and talking quietly.)*

BUD. I say we distract him, then hit him with a fireplace tool.

DAD. We don't have a fireplace.

BUD. ...We could crack the candy dish over his head.

UNCLE LEO. Too light – *somebody* emptied it.

DAD. Leo, don't start – we need to work together.

BUD. None o' this woulda happened if you people hunted. Nothin' says "Keep Out" like an NRA sticker in your window.

UNCLE LEO. *(sarcastically)* Maybe you could hit him with your bowling ball...

BUD. Listen – I've had about enough –

DAD. *(to BUD)* Stop it. *(to UNCLE LEO)* Stop it. You two have got to quit arguing and figure out a way to end this.

PAUL. There's one of him and three of you – why don't you just jump him?

UNCLE LEO. And what are you gonna do – sit there and take pictures. You're a part o' this too.

PAUL. I don't believe in violence.

BUD. Naturally.

> *(They suddenly get quiet as TONY enters the room.)*

TONY. What are yous doin'?

BUD. Nothin'.

TONY. Then why do ya look guilty?

BUD. *(thinks)* I'm supposed to be on a diet, and I ate all this candy and...

DAD. He's feeling bad.

UNCLE LEO. The man's racked with guilt.

PAUL. We're just trying to help him through it.

TONY. You are without a doubt, the *weirdest* family I have ever met.

UNCLE LEO. We try.

TONY. Do us all a favor and stop tryin'. Just sit there and don't make a sound.

BUD. Uh, I don't wanna sound like an idiot –

UNCLE LEO. Then don't speak.

BUD. (*gives* **UNCLE LEO** *a dirty look*) –but, I was wonderin'... just what exactly did you guys do? Why are th' cops after ya?

TONY. What's it to yas?

BUD. Just curious.

TONY. We needed a little extra cash and thought that we'd make an easy score on Christmas Eve. Figured there wouldn't be many cops out on account o' th' snow.

DAD. And your getaway plan was to hide out in a neighborhood?

TONY. No. The plan was to drive away.

DAD. So did you really smash into somebody's fountain?

TONY. Of course not – the car wouldn't start –s o we ran away on foot.

UNCLE LEO. Wouldn't the police just follow your tracks in the snow back to your car?

TONY. I never went back to th' car.

DAD. I'm confused. If you never went back to the car – how do you know it wouldn't start?

TONY. Vinny was waitin' in th' car and it died on him as he was sittin' there.

BUD. Your getaway car died?!

TONY. Bum luck, huh? ...Anyways, I told him to run in the opposite direction and meet me two blocks down. That's when we headed this way.

DAD. What made you pick this house?

TONY. Yer neighbors over there had an A.D.T. sign in th' yard, and th' ones on dat side had an NRA sticker in th' back window of their car.

BUD. What'd I say?!

UNCLE LEO. Never mind him – he's been blabbin' like an idiot since he blew the whole diet thing. Actually, he's been blabbin' like an idiot for as long as I've known him.

(AUNT ROSE enters from the hall bathroom.)

AUNT ROSE. Leo stop bein' rude.

UNCLE LEO. Who's bein' rude? I'm tellin' th' truth.

AUNT ROSE. Never mind him, Bud – he's get's grumpy when he's constipated.

TONY. Lady – what's yer name? Rose – Get in th' other room and quit startin' stuff.

AUNT ROSE. *(mocking UNCLE LEO)* Who's startin' stuff? I'm speakin' th' truth…

(She exits.)

UNCLE LEO. If you ever wonder why polar bears eat their young – there's your answer.

(The lights fade down on the living room and again the men freeze as the lights come up and the action restores in the dining room.)

EMILY. He did not!

MRS. WAKOWSKI. Oh yes. When your father was younger, he was quite the Romeo.

BUNNY. *(to TRACY)* So was your father.

TRACY. Nuh uh.

BUNNY. Oh yeah – he knew how to get a girl's attention.

AUNT ROSE. Next.

TRACY. Hang on – they're telling us romantic stories about our dads.

AUNT ROSE. Your dad was a pistol when he was younger.

MRS. WAKOWSKI. I'm sorry, I've been doing all the talking – Tell us something romantic that Bud did.

BUNNY. Well, when I was in high school, I played on the volleyball team. Bud and a bunch of his friends would come to every game – home and away. This one night, he and his buddies painted their chests to spell out "Tigers" – the name of our mascot. But then came the sweetest surprise. During the first time-out, as we were walkin' toward the bench – he turned around, and he'd shaved a big heart and my initials in his back hair!

BETH. Nothing says romance like back-hair art.

VINNY. *(after a long pause)* I can hardly scratch my shoulder blades – I wonder how he reached back there to shave it?

BUNNY. Excuse me, girls – I've gotta make a little pit stop. *(She exits to the restroom.)*

VINNY. This is really great information I'm learnin' today. Maybe this'll help me get a date.

BETH. Let me give you some more valuable info: don't rob stores – prison is a lousy place to pick up chicks.

TRACY. Isn't this interesting?

BETH. Stories about the disgusting things our parents did to get each other's attention?!?

TRACY. No – the way that we are working through the levels of H.C.I.S.

VINNY. Th' what?

TRACY. H.C.I.S. Hostage-Captor Identification Syndrome. I did a report on it last year and we are fitting the mold perfectly!

MRS. WAKOWSKI. What are you talking about?

TRACY. There's this psychological syndrome that associated with hostages and their captors and it's really interesting.

BETH. Now, I know why she has a 4.15.

TRACY. When a person is taken hostage, they go through various stages mentally. In the first stage: the hostages start to feel positive about their captors.

VINNY. That's nice.

TRACY. It's how they block out the notion that they might actually die!

AUNT ROSE. Lovely.

TRACY. In stage two, the hostages start to develop negative feelings toward the people whom are responsible for their rescue – especially if they are held for a long time. They feel let down and abandoned.

AUNT ROSE. Sounds like my marriage to Leo.

MRS. WAKOWSKI. It's fascinating that you remember all this.

TRACY. I love learning!

BETH. What is wrong with you?!

yeek

VINNY. What is the next stage?

FINAL STAGE

TRACY. The third stage is the final one. It's where the captors begin to have positive feelings about their hostages.

VINNY. I don't think Tony's there yet.

MRS. WAKOWSKI. I'm pretty sure you're right.

VINNY. He's a good guy – today just didn't work out quite the way he had planned.

(**BUNNY** *returns from the bathroom.*)

BUNNY. What'd I miss?

MRS. WAKOWSKI. Tracy has been explaining – what do you call it?

TRACY. H.C.I.S. – the "hostage captor identification syndrome." It's a theory about how hostages and their captors start to identify with each other.

BUNNY. Like Vinny wantin' to know more about how Bud and I met?

TRACY. Exactly.

BUNNY. Wow – that's really interesting.

(**TONY** *appears in the doorway.*)

TONY. What's goin' on?

VINNY. Nothin' we're just talkin.'

(**TONY** *throws up his hands in disbelief.*)

What is yer deal? A few minutes ago you was upset 'cause they was too quiet.

BETH. We're willing to compromise – we could all mumble.

TONY. I thought it was bad havin' yous all in the same room, but it ain't no better havin' ya apart. Bud and Leo are acting like a couple o' five year olds –

AUNT ROSE. (*to* **MRS. WAKOWSKI**) Oh good – he's aged a year.

TONY. I don't know how you twos do it – but yous deserve some kinda medal for stayin' married to those crackpots.

BUNNY. Finally, someone truly understands...

VINNY. Hey Tony – I'm getting' a little stir crazy. Can we move rooms or somethin'?

TONY. I'm ready ta move houses –

BETH. It's been great having you – g'bye.

TONY. Hardy har har. (*to* **VINNY**) We can just trade places. You go to th' toddler room for a while and I'll swim in the estrogen tank.

VINNY. Sounds good ta me.

(*He exits.*)

MRS. WAKOWSKI. How long are you prepared to stay?

TONY. All night if that's what it takes.

BETH. (*dripping with sarcasm*) Oh boy – a sleep over.

TONY. Do you ever make anything other than smart comments?!

BETH. Never. I leave the stupid ones to you.

(*Lights fade to black in the dining room and come up in the living room.*)

BUD. What's this?

VINNY. I was getting' a little crazy in there –

UNCLE LEO. Time with Rose does that to me too.

DAD. Leo, if you'd give her a break every now and then –

UNCLE LEO. Oh, I've considered givin' her a couple of breaks through the years…

BUD. Yeah, only you knew she'd dust you like White House furniture!

VINNY. Hey now – we ain't havin' that. Those ladies is in there sayin' the nicest things about yous that's ever been told. What are you doin'? Yer in here trashin' 'em. If yer not gonna say nice things, then shut up.

(There is a long pause as **UNCLE LEO** *and* **BUD** *each start to say something, but realize it's going to be rude so they sit uncomfortably.)*

BUD. Hey Vinny?

VINNY. Yeah?

BUD. What's in the bag?

VINNY. It's the take.

BUD. From the robbery?

UNCLE LEO. No from th – *(realizes he's about to say something rude and stops, then pretends to zip his lip)*

BUD. Have you counted it yet?

VINNY. No, we ain't had no chance ta even look at it.

BUD. We got plenty o' time right now.

VINNY. *(uneasy)* I don't know…Tony'd prob'ly get mad.

UNCLE LEO. In that case – we won't tell him. Dump it out.

*(***VINNY*** looks around and then dumps the bag on the couch.)*

Hey, you guys did alright. There must be three or four hundred dollars here.

BUD. *(crosses from chair)* Hey, they stiffed you – there's some play money in here!

UNCLE LEO. That ain't play money, Bud – it's an old silver certificate. They're pretty valuable.

DAD. Wow, let me get a look at that.

PAUL. That's really cool.

*(***UNCLE LEO*** stands to hand the bill to* **DAD**, *but as he reaches out with it, he gets the bill too close to the candle on the table and the bill instantly goes up in smoke.)*

BUD. *(can't resist)* What's it worth now?

VINNY. Hey, where'd that bill go?!

BUD. Search me.

VINNY. Why, do you have it on yas?

BUD. ...No, that's just a figure o' speech...

VINNY. Whatever yous do – don't mention a word o' dat ta Tony!

DAD. So what's the deal with Tony? You seem like a nice enough young man – how'd you get mixed up with him?

VINNY. Tony? He's a good guy –

PAUL. – That just happens to enjoy robbery.

VINNY. This is the first time he ever robbed anything.

DAD. Are you kidding us?

VINNY. No – it's the truth. He just had ta do it on account o' his situation.

DAD. What *situation* – that's the second time you've said that?

VINNY. Ahhh, he wouldn't want me sayin' nothin' about it.

UNCLE LEO. C'mon, you can't throw that out there and not tell us. What's his situation?

VINNY. If I tell yous – ya gotta swear Tony won't find out.

UNCLE LEO. You got it.

BUD. Scout's promise.

VINNY. *(looks around nervously)* Tony, he had a real good job. He was a parts manager at one o' th' big GM dealerships on Long Island. That is til the economy started tankin'. Sales were slumpin' and they was layin' people off left and right, and Tony'd been there a long time so he was alright. Then when the President started bailin' out the automakers he said they had ta close a buncha shops. That's when Tony got hit. He lost his job and then his house. He an' his wife and kids moved out ta Jersey and he's been lookin' for work ever since. He didn't rob that store cause he's a crook – he just wanted ta be able to buy somethin' nice for his two boys for Christmas.

(The lights slow fade to black and then come up in the dining room.)

BUNNY. Tony.

TONY. What?

BUNNY. I think it's time for the ladies to switch as well.

TONY. What?

AUNT ROSE. These seats are hard on an antique booty.

BUNNY. We just realized that the men are all in there lounging around on comfortable chairs while we're in here suffering.

TONY. Sufferin'?! – Yous ain't th' ones sufferin'!!

EMILY. Try one of these seats then.

TONY. You people are unbelievable. Nothin' satisfies you! First ya gotta have the dinin' room cuz th' men'll eat everything in th' room – now yous gotta have the livin' room cuz th' men got all the good chairs. I'm the one wit' pain in the butt – and it's you people!!

BUNNY. So does that mean we can go?

(TONY throws up his hands in surrender. They smile and head for the door.)

AUNT ROSE. Get up Leo and make way for th' ladies.

BUNNY. *(to BUD)* You too.

(There is a commotion outside the door and TONY panics.)

TONY. Everybody shut up and get down!!! You *(points to BETH)* Go to th' window and see who that is.

(She crosses to window where we can faintly see MRS. DRAPER peeking in. BETH doesn't see her.)

BETH. It's Christmas Carolers.

(We hear them begin to sing "Hark The Herald Angel Sings")

BUD. It's what?

BETH. Christmas Carolers!

TONY. Get rid of 'em.

BETH. How?

TONY. I don't care – just get rid of 'em!

BETH. I don't know how to –

DAD. Beth – just get them to go away!

BETH. Fine!

(She crosses to door, opens it and screams.)

We're Jewish!!!

(The carolers abruptly stop and shuffle off.)

DAD. Are you crazy!?

BETH. You said get rid of them.

DAD. I didn't mean offend them.

BETH. If we were Jewish – they'd be offending *us*.

DAD: But we're *not* Jewish *(He looks out the window.)* and they know it! They're from our church!!

BETH. Well, you've been saying you might want to try another fellowship…

DAD. Beth!

BETH. Listen – I said I didn't know what to do and you said it didn't matter just get rid of 'em – so I did. If you don't like the way I do things, then next time you take care of it!!!

TONY. SHUT UP! Both of yas!! I've had all I'm gonna –

*(As **TONY** focuses on **BETH** and **DAD**, **BUD** hits **TONY** across the back, and wrestles the gun away from him.)*

BUD. *(to **TONY**)* Back off!!! How do ya like me now, Leo! We ain't hostages anymore, and you two are goin' to jail. Tom, get the money bag. Bunny – call the cops.

*(Suddenly the door bursts open, and it is **MRS. DRAPER** and she is wielding a large snow shovel.)*

MRS. DRAPER. There'll be no robberies in this neighborhood! *(She pulls back the shovel to hit **BUD**.)*

DAD. No Sue – wait!!

(She hits **BUD** *with the butt of the shovel in the mid-section. As he crumples over, she strikes him across the back with the scoop end of the shovel and he falls to the floor. The pistol slides harmlessly over to* **TONY***'s feet.)*

UNCLE LEO. *(to* **BUD***)* You still want me to answer your question?

TONY. *(picks up gun and speaks to* **MRS. DRAPER***)* Thanks a lot lady. Now get over there wit' th' others.

MRS. DRAPER. *(confused, to* **DAD***)* What's he doing Thomas?

DAD. He's holding you hostage.

MRS. DRAPER. *(points to* **BUD***)* I thought *he* was holding *you* hostage?

DAD. No, that my brother-in-law, Bud – you met his wife Bunny earlier.

MRS. DRAPER. Oh, no…

BETH. Oh, yes.

DAD. Right idea – wrong victim. You alright Bud?

BUD. *(in falsetto voice)* I'll be fine…right after I throw up.

VINNY. Boy Tony, dat was close.

TONY. Too close. Look, maybe yous guys done got comfortable or somethin' –

VINNY. They're in stage one.

TONY. What?

VINNY. It's this whole theory Tracy was tellin' us about how–

TONY. *(to* **VINNY***)* I DON'T CARE! *(to group)* Let me make myself clear: I *will* shoot yous if I have to. Now sit down and don't make a peep.

AUNT ROSE. Oh, I looove peeps – especially the pink ones.

EMILY. I like the little yellow chicks –

TONY. *(with authority)* SIT. DOWN.

BUNNY. There aren't enough seats –

TONY. Then use the one God gave yas!!!

(They all scramble to find places on the floor.)

Vinny, I need ta see yous in th' dinin' room. *(They exit.)* This is startin' ta get serious – that was too close. How many bullets ya got?

VINNY. Bullets?

TONY. Yeah, for yas pistol.

VINNY. *(sheepish)* Uh…none.

TONY. None! – You forgot to load it?!

VINNY. *(pulls out water gun)* No, it's a water pistol.

TONY. *(trying to stay quiet)* A water pistol! Are you an idiot?!?

VINNY. Well, I knew you was bringin' a gun an' I didn't see no point in both of us getting' armed robbery raps –

TONY. Great, so yous hung me out ta dry.

VINNY. Actually, I need to hang *me* out ta dry 'cause this thing leaked all over the place while I was waitin' for yas. It got on my crotch and made it look like I'd peed myself.

TONY. You are a real piece o' work, you know that!? All this time I thought yous had my back – and yer carryin' a water pistol! Get in there an' make sure that everybody thinks yer armed and dangerous.

(They both exit into the living room.)

BUNNY. Do you think we could go back to the –

TONY and **VINNY.** NO!

BUNNY. Just thought I'd ask…

*(The dining room door opens, and we see **JANET** appear. She crosses to the living room doorway behind **TONY**.)*

JANET. Why's everyone crammed in the living room?

TONY. *(spooked, he jumps)* WHOA–Holy cow! – Who are you!!!

JANET. I live here…who are *you*?

TONY. How'd yous get in here?

JANET. I came in through the back door. The front stoop hasn't been shoveled. Would someone please explain to me what's going on?

(Everyone begins to speak all at once and it turns to chaos. **TONY** *just shakes his head and* **VINNY** *looks overwhelmed.)*

Hold it… Hold it… HOLD IT! I can't understand a thing if you're all talking at the same time! Tom?…

DAD. To make a long and twisted story, short and simple: This is Tony, that's Vinny – and they are holding us hostage.

JANET. They're what?

DAD. Holding us hostage.

JANET. *(laughing)* Oh, that's funny…who are they really?

BETH. It's no joke, Mom. We're stuck with them.

JANET. Oh c'mon – who are you?

TONY. Lady, are yous dense or somethin'? *(He pulls out his pistol.)*

JANET. O-kay. Why are you here?…

(Again, everyone starts to tell the story from their point of view and chaos ensues.)

TONY. For th' love o' Christmas – you people are mind-numbing! *(to* **DAD***)* You…You done great a minute ago – give her the *Reader's Digest* version.

DAD. They robbed a store, their getaway car didn't work, they fled on foot, needed a place to hide, picked our house. *(to* **TONY***)* Is that pretty much it?

TONY. Perfect.

JANET. Why our house?

BUD. 'Cause you don't own any guns.

JANET. How did you know that?

VINNY. No N.R.A. stickers in yer car windows.

*(***BUD*** sits looking smug.)*

JANET. So has anybody eaten?

BUNNY. We took care o' everything. Everyone's eaten and we even made a plate for you. *(***BUNNY*** starts to get up.)* You want me to microwave it for you?

TONY. Whoa, whoa, whoa – sit down, Bunny.

AUNT ROSE. She's been in Vermont all day waiting at an airport to get home for Christmas Eve.

EMILY. And now you're not gonna let her eat?!

MRS. WAKOWSKI. The poor woman's probably worn out.

MRS. DRAPER. And those cheap-skate airlines won't even give you peanuts anymore! …Unless you fly first class like Theodore and I.

TRACY. That's pretty low –

PAUL. Yeah, even for a *criminal.*

TONY. Alright already – yous guys should be lawyers.

> *(**BUNNY** starts to get up, when the doorbell rings.)*

> Who now???!!! We've got everybody but th' Pope in here!

VINNY. I doubt if it's him – they're Jewish…

JANET. What?!

DAD. It's a long story.

TONY. Look out th' window – who is it?

DAD. Uh…

TONY: Who is it?

DAD: …it's a Police officer.

VINNY. Uh oh Tony – uh oh. This ain't good.

TONY. *(trying not to panic)* Everybody relax and look natural. We're just one big happy family…

VINNY. One *really big* happy family… *(to **BETH**)* Except you. You're not so happy…

TONY. Hey yappy – could you shut up and blend in? Open the door and don't pull anything.

> *(The doorbell rings and **DAD** crosses and opens the door. He instantly recognizes the policeman.)*

DAD. Officer Henley, how are you?

OFFICER. Fine Tom. You?

DAD. Doing very well. Merry Christmas Eve.

OFFICER. Same to you. Could I come in for a minute?

DAD. Sure, come on in.

(He enters and is taken aback at the large number of people in the room.)

OFFICER. Wow, you've got quite a crowd.

DAD. It's our annual family Christmas gathering.

OFFICER. Smells good – Janet, did you do all the cooking?

JANET. *(hesitates for a moment)* ...Oh, no...I had some help. I just did the green beans. Beth and Tom did the ham.

BUD. Bunny did the carrot cake.

UNCLE LEO. Rose did the mashed potatoes.

BETH. Wentworth did the Macarena.

(They all look mortified.)

OFFICER. Excuse me?

BETH. Ooops, I meant the macaroni.

OFFICER. Listen, I'm really sorry to interrupt your family meal, but I'm here on official business.

BETH. *(mock ignorance)* Did we do something wrong?

DAD. Beth, I'll handle this. Did we do something wrong.

OFFICER. There was a robbery nearby about three hours ago and the suspect fled on foot. We have reason to believe that he may have an accomplice and that they may be hiding out in a residence.

AUNT ROSE. Do you have a description of the suspects? *(She looks straight at* **TONY.***)*

OFFICER. Not really. The only person that actually saw the gunman was the store clerk and she's a little near-sighted. She thinks he had on a blue coat.

BUD. What'd he steal?

OFFICER. He got away with a sack of money.

(There is a slight pause as we see **DAD** *start to smile.)*

DAD. Wow...now it's all starting to come together.

OFFICER. In what way?

DAD. Well, my cousins – Wentworth and Vincent – were a little late getting to dinner...

OFFICER. And...??

DAD. And when they were walking up the drive – they saw this sack laying under our shrubs. Where did we put that, Leo?

UNCLE LEO. Here it is. *(passes it to* **OFFICER HENLEY***)*

DAD. Wentworth – where did you put that pistol that was in the bag?

(There is a long silence as **TONY** *stares at* **DAD** *trying to decide his next move.)*

TONY. *(playing along)* I put it in my coat – I didn't want th' kids gettin' a hold of it.

OFFICER. Sir, can I see the weapon please.

*(***TONY** *reaches slowly into his coat and pulls out the pistol, he is considering doing something, then* **DAD** *cuts him off.)*

DAD. Oh no – I hope we didn't ruin any evidence. It's got his fingerprints on it – we didn't think about a robbery.

OFFICER. Well, best case scenario would have been for you to have left it in the bag so we could dust for prints, but –

DAD. Well, it was down under the money and we didn't know what it was until we reached in the bag and touched it. By then it was too late.

OFFICER. I see. *(He looks at* **TONY** *for a moment, then addresses* **DAD**.*)* And you can verify his identity?

DAD. Absolutely. Wentworth Douglas – he's my cousin on my mother's side.

OFFICER. Please to meet you, Mr. Douglas. Where exactly was the bag when you first spotted it?

TONY. *(changes voice, trying to sound like a "Wentworth")* Well Officer...as Thomas said – it was down behind the shrubbery.

OFFICER. Can you show me out the window?

TONY. Certainly. *(points)* It was that bush right there.

OFFICER. The one with the multi-colored lights?

TONY. Exactly.

(As this exchange is taking place – they are all staring in disbelief as **TONY** *makes up the story and* **DAD** *does nothing to indicate that* **TONY** *is the criminal.)*

TONY. *(cont.)* If I hadn't dropped my keys and bent down in the snow to get them – I probably wouldn't have even seen the bag.

OFFICER. Did you happen to see anyone while you were out there?

TONY. *(points to* **MRS. DRAPER***)* Only their helpful neighbor here – Mrs. Draper.

OFFICER. Sue, did you see anyone?

(She glances at **VINNY** *who points his finger at her under his coat.)*

MRS. DRAPER. No, Michael – I didn't see a soul…

OFFICER. Well, this is a great piece of evidence. I certainly appreciate your help.

DAD. It was my pleasure.

OFFICER. I hate to do this, but we'll need to send our CSI unit to check for other evidence in your yard.

JANET. What sort of evidence?

OFFICER. Tracks in the snow, dropped articles, that sort of thing.

*(***TONY*** tenses up.)*

DAD. The way it's been snowing, I don't think there'll be any footprints to see.

OFFICER. I'm afraid you're right.

TONY. *(***TONY*** looks out window.)* Yeah, there's a lot more snow than when we first picked this place. *(realizes what he said)*

OFFICER. Excuse me?

TONY. I said there's a lot more snow than when we picked up this in the first place. *(holds up the money sack)*

OFFICER. Can we count on your cooperation with the investigation if we have further questions?

TONY. Without a doubt, Officer.

OFFICER. Listen folks, I won't waste any more of your family time. *(to* **DAD***)* If we need to speak with your cousin again – I'll call and get his contact information from you.

DAD. Sounds great. I hope you guys are able to catch this guy.

OFFICER. We'll do our best.

DAD. Be careful out there and have a great holiday.

OFFICER. Thank you – and I apologize again for the interruption – good night.

(**DAD** *closes the door. They all stare in disbelief at* **DAD.**)

MRS. WAKOWSKI. Are you crazy?!?

MRS. DRAPER. You could've turned these hooligans in to police and instead you *lie* to the officer?!?

BETH. Why in the world didn't you end this?

DAD. I did end it.

BUNNY. How do you figure?

DAD. Tony doesn't have a gun. The police have the money.

TRACY. Yeah, but –

DAD. I vouched for his identity and his whereabouts.

AUNT ROSE. But why??

DAD. Don't you see: it's perfect. It's like it never happened.

BUD. I never thought that – it's like they get a do-over.

UNCLE LEO. Yeah, a mulligan –

UNCLE LEO/BUD. *(together)* Like in golf.

(**UNCLE LEO** *turns and stares at* **BUD.**)

BUD. What? You think bowling is the only sport I know?

UNCLE LEO: Bowling is *not* a sport –

(**AUNT ROSE** *jabs him in the ribcage to shut him up.*)

JANET. I'm lost – so explain to me why you didn't tell the officer?

VINNY. Yeah, why'd you do that?

TONY. You had the chance – why didn't you turn us in?

DAD. Why didn't you shoot us when *you* had the chance?

TONY. I didn't wanna hurt nobody.

DAD. And I didn't want to hurt you. Vinny told us why you robbed that store. I don't see any point in kicking a man when he's down.

TONY. *(gets very quiet)* It's not what I deserve.

DAD. An undeserved gift – isn't that what "the Christmas spirit" is all about?

BUNNY. What do you mean by his "situation?"

BUD. Tony's been out o' work for a long time.

UNCLE LEO. They were robbing the store so he could buy his two sons Christmas presents.

TRACY. That's the sweetest thing I ever heard.

DAD. He has a three year-old and five year-old – right?

TONY. *(quietly)* Yeah.

JANET. *(crosses to tree, taking charge)* Well, my sister has two boys the same ages and they're not coming til next Tuesday. *(She starts passing presents out from under the tree.)* So, you can take these for your boys and we'll get new ones before they get here.

VINNY. *(emotional)* This is the best Christmas present I ever got. *(hugs* **MRS. DRAPER***)*

TONY. You people are unbelievable. *(extends his hand to shake)* Thank you. Mr. Douglas, really…thank yous… but I just got one question.

DAD. Yeah?

TONY. Why weren't you worried about Vinny's gun?

DAD. Earlier, when he raised his hand to ask a question, his coat rode up and I noticed the wet spot on his pants.

VINNY. You saw that? – I'm so embarrassed!

DAD. Don't be. The plastic handle was sticking out of your pocket and I figured it was a water pistol you were carrying.

VINNY. You guys are geniuses! Merry Christmas.

DAD. *(extends his hand to shake again)* Merry Christmas.

EVERYONE. Merry Christmas.

(fade to black)

(As the curtain opens for Curtain Call, the carolers come out first singing "We Wish You A Merry Christmas." After the first stanza – **BETH** *appears from behind the proscenium.)*

BETH. *(waving to get their attention)* Okay, you got your moment in the spotlight – now shut up so we can bow!!!

(begin cast bows)

(curtain)

END OF SHOW

PROPERTY LIST

ACT ONE

Scene One: Christmas tree fully decorated, presents, assorted holiday decor, hair brush, apron, cell phone, trivet, large pot with cooked ham, meat thermometer, small area rugs, china, tableware, glasses, cloth napkins, candlesticks/candles, Zip-loc with sugar

Scene Two: Pyrex dishes with food, punch glasses, punch, presents/gift bags, pipe (Leo)

Scene Three: pistol, money sack, large oven mitt, basket with rolls, apron, serving spoon, platter with ham, electric knife, serving fork, can of Dr. Pepper

ACT TWO

Scene One: two small Christmas gift bags, carrot cake, dessert plates, forks, cake knife, coffee, coffee cups, coffee pot

Scene Two: candy dish, assorted candy, coffee, cups, snack food, tissues (Vinny)

Scene Three: candle, stage money, flash paper cash (for special effect), silver certificate, snow shovel, water pistol, rolling suitcase, tablet and pen (Office Henley), sack, pistol, gifts

COSTUME PLOT

DAD: khaki slacks, button-down oxford shirt, Hush Puppy shoes, belt, apron

BETH: jeans, stylish sweater, cute shoes

MRS. DRAPER: beautiful dress coat, pant suit, high-heeled boots, fur hat, scarf, gloves

BUNNY: brightly colored winter coat, denim jumper, holiday tights, red shoes/boots, Santa hat, tacky holiday jewelry

BUD: barn coat, work boots, Carhartt pants, flannel shirt, sleeveless undershirt, camo cap

TRACY: ski jacket, thick sweater, jeans, snowboots

AUNT ROSE: fur coat, slacks, blouse, loud shoes, flashy jewelry

UNCLE LEO: fedora, wool trench coat, long-sleeve dress shirt, ascot, sweater vest, expensive slacks, white shoes

TONY: navy pea coat, worn khakis, work boots, long sleeve henley, black stocking cap

VINNY: O.D. green army field jacket, gray sweatshirt, blue jeans, hunting boots, Yankess cap

PAUL: zippered and hooded sweatshirt, goth shirt, slashed blue jeans, combat boots, dog collar

EMILY: ski coat, colorful sweater, jeans, boots

MRS. WAKOWSKI: hooded winter coat, slacks, blouse, scarf, boots

CHRISTMAS CAROLERS: winter coats, scarves, hats, boots, gloves

MOM: wool over-coat, dress suit, stylish boots and scarf

OFFICER HENLEY: winter over-coat, hat, police uniform, tactical boots and gloves

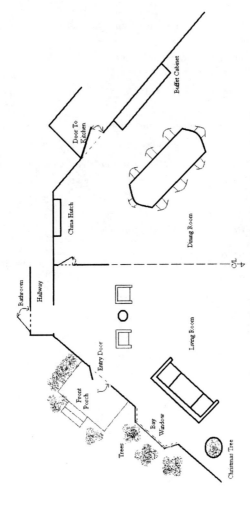

SCENE DESIGN FOR "IN-LAWS, OUTLAWS & OTHER PEOPLE THAT SHOULD BE SHOT"

Image appears courtesy of the author.

OTHER TITLES AVAILABLE FROM SAMUEL FRENCH

FOUR WEDDINGS AND AN ELVIS

Nancy Frick

Comedy / 7m, 4f / Interior Set

Sandy, the four-times-married-three-times-divorced owner of a wedding chapel in Las Vegas, has certainly seen her fair share of matrimonies! In the hilarious Four Weddings and an Elvis, we witness four of her funniest: Bev and Stan, who are getting married – by the King himself – as revenge on their exes; Vanessa and Bryce, two arrogant aging stars who are tying the knot as a publicity ploy, and are vexed by an aging Elvis who doesn't know who they are; and Martin and Fiona, a gentle postal-worker and a tough ex-con trying to get married before the police arrive! However, the final wedding is the funniest all: Sandy's fifth and final wedding which reveals a hilarious twist! With simple scenic requirements and memorable characters, Four Weddings and an Elvis is a comedic treat certain to please audiences!

"Come enjoy four acts of love...or something like it. What happens in Las Vegas...is hilarious!" – *Eventful*

"Laughter abounded throughout the play on opening night.... Not only were expectations met, they were exceeded!" – *Montgomery Media*

"Screechingly funny!" – *Phillyfun Journal*

CPSIA information can be obtained at www.ICGtesting.com
Printed in the USA
BVOW01s1020240913

331995BV00014B/350/P